A Story a Day

365

stories and rhymes for Girls

Illustrated by Eva Musynski, Marina le Ray, Veronica Vasylenko and Hannah Wood.

Additional illustrations by Simone Abel, Maddy Bell, Alex Burnett, Caroline Jayne Church, Jacqueline East, Chris Embleton, Frances Evans, June Goulding, Anna C. Leplar, Sanja Rescek, Kirsten Richards, Kristina Stephenson, Sara Walker and Michelle White.

Written by Cecil Frances Alexander, William Allingham, Hans Christian Andersen, Kay Barnes, Tina Barrett, William Blake, Jane Euphemia Brown, Moira Butterfield, Deborah Chancellor, Andy Charman, Nick Ellsworth, Gaby Goldsack, Jillian Harker, Karen Hayles, Liz Holliday, Thomas Hood, Lizzie Irvin, John Keats, Charles Kingsley, Edward Lear, Ingrid Maitland, Susan Nicholson, Beatrice Phillpotts, Ronne Randall, Sandy Ransford, Caroline Repchuck, Debbie Rivers-Moore, Beth Roberts, William Roscoe, Christina Rossetti, Anna Sewell, William Shakespeare, Louisa Somerville, Robert Louis Stevenson, Christine Tagg, Jane Taylor, Alfred, Lord Tennyson and Gordon Volke.

Every effort has been made to acknowledge the contributors to this book. If we have made any errors, we will be pleased to rectify them in future editions.

This edition published by Parragon in 2011

Parragon
Queen Street House
4 Queen Street
Bath BA1 1HE, UK

ISBN 978-1-4454-5497-9

Printed in China

A Story a Day

365

stories and
rhymes
for Girls

PaRragon

Bath • New York • Singapore • Hong Kong • Cologne • Delhi
Melbourne • Amsterdam • Johannesburg • Auckland • Shenzhen

Contents

The Soccer Fairy. 10
One Snowy Day. 12
Elsie Elephant's Jungle
    Shower. 13
There Was an Old Man
from Peru 14
I Eat My Peas with
    Honey 14
Haymaking 14
The Old Woman's
    Three Cows 15
Sing, Sing. 15
To the Snail 15
The Easter Bunny 16
Bertha Saves the Day 17
Thank You, Kitty. 18
You Can Do It, Kitty 19
The Princess and the Pea 20
Roses Are Red 24
Little Poll Parrot 24
I Had a Little Horse. 24
The Legacy. 25
Sowing Corn. 25
Small Is the Wren. 25
Jalissa and the Jewels 26
Bella Bunny's Bonnet 28
Brave Billy Bunny. 29
Kiana and the Butterfly 30
Home Sweet Home 31
Rufus the Farm Kitten. 32
A Hat Like That 34

Ariel's Song 36
A Frog He Would
    a-Wooing Go 36
A Candle 36
A Tisket, a Tasket 37
My Black Hen 37
I Had a Little Hen. 37
The Mischievous Mermaids 38
Two Princesses 40
The Littlest Frog 42
Baby Bear's Friend. 43
Don't Be Shy, Suzy 44
Suzy Helps Out 45
Oh, Bear! 46
Clumsy Fairy 48
The Yellow Harebells 49
Maria's Haircut 50
Sunshine. 52
Mrs. Hen 52
Thaw 52
Little Boy Blue. 53
Billy and Me 53
Little Nag 53
Sugarplum and the Butterfly . , ... 54
The Elves and the Shoemaker 56
Kiss It Better 58
Helpful Baby Elephant 60
Sleepy Baby Tiger 61
Maxine to the Rescue. 62
Hurt No Living Thing 64
The Great Brown Owl. 65

Contents

Mousie 66

Mrs. Mason's Basin 66

Ride a Cock Horse 66

Grandma's Glasses 67

Tickly, Tickly. 67

Build a House with Five Bricks 67

Little Red Riding Hood 68

Two Little Kittens 72

Princess Sleepyhead 73

Slow Down, Max 74

Jacob, the Shyest Rabbit 76

Small and Pink 78

The Emperor's New Clothes 80

Little Miss Muffet. 84

Little Jumping Joan. 84

There Was a Little Girl 84

Anna Maria. 85

Round-eared Cap. 85

Goldy Locks, Goldy Locks. 85

I Love My Puppy 86

I Love My Kitten 87

I Love My Pony 88

I Love My Bunny 89

The Ugly Duckling 90

Hamster Sleepover. 94

Silly Millie Jarter 96

The Broom Song 96

Cock Crow 96

Chairs to Mend 97

Puss in the Pantry 97

My Maid Mary 97

The Owl and the Pussycat. 98

Ten in the Bed 99

The Rainy Day 100

Spring. 102

All the Bells Were Ringing 103

The Gossips 104

Engine, Engine. 104

Buff. 104

Puss at the Door. 105

Three Ghostesses 105

Laundry Day 105

The Ant and the Grasshopper. 106

Amber and the Flowers 108

Hazel Squirrel 110

The Dragon Who Was

    Scared of Flying. 112

Thank You 114

Cock Robin's Courtship 114

Grig's Pig 114

Little Betty Blue 115

See-saw, Margery Daw 116

Elsie Marley 115

The Swing 115

City Child 117

Copycat Max 118

Forever Friends 119

My Grandpa Is Great 120

Snow White 122

Mary, Mary, Quite Contrary 126

A Nickel. 126

Here Comes a Widow 126

Jack Sprat's Cat 127

Butterfly. 127

An Egg. 127

Grumpy Fairy 128

The Little Doll 130

Skipping. 131

Lion's Birthday 132
Sad Monkey. 133
Surprise Sleepover 134
Minnie and Mattie. 136
Meg Merrilees 137
There Was an Old Woman
    Who Lived in a Shoe. 138
There Was an Old Woman
    Tossed Up in a Basket. 139
My Grandma Is Great. 140
Lucy Locket 142
Ice Cream. 142
If Pigs Could Fly 142
The Wind. 143
Kindness. 143
Little Friend 143
Cinderella. 144
Bunny Helps Mommy 148
Pajama Party Disco. 150
The Fairies 152
The Butterfly's Ball 153
Just as Well, Really! 154
Clara Cow's Cold 155
Utterly Crazy. 156
The Cherry Tree 156
The Apple Tree. 156
I Had a Little Nut Tree 157
Little Fishes 157
Ickle Ockle. 157
I'm a Big Sister!. 158
A Friend for Barney 162
Nibbling Neighbors. 164
My Mother Said 166
Bed in Summer. 167

Snoozy Princess Susie 168
Birthday Sleepover. 170
The Enchanted Garden 172
Can I See Another's Woe? 174
Bob Robin 174
Old Farmer Giles 174
Red Stockings. 175
Fidget. 175
The Dove Says 175
Dreams. 176
Three Little Kittens 177
My Dad Is Great 178
An Angel of My Own 180
The Seasons 184
The Moon. 185
In Lincoln Lane 186
Charley Barley. 186
Five Little Ducks 186
There Was an Old Crow 187
Birds of a Feather. 187
The Wise Old Owl. 187
Sleepover Splash. 188
Mina's Lucky Shoes 190
Good Girl, Molly 192
Goldy and the Jacket 193
Fishes Swim 194
Feathers 194
Cut Thistles 194
Pussycat and Robin 195
Robin and Pussycat. 195
Three Blind Mice 195
Bedtime 196
Hush, Little Baby 197
The Case of the

Contents

Disappearing Books 198

Perfect Pony 200

Oranges and Lemons 204

London Bells. 204

My Little Cow 205

Jemmy Dawson 205

I See the Moon 205

For Every Evil Under the Sun 205

Juanita's Big Chance 206

Let's Play! 208

This Is Fun! 209

Twinkle, Twinkle 210

Sleep, Baby, Sleep 211

My Best Friend. 212

Frère Jacques 216

O Lady Moon. 216

Ding, Dong, Bell 216

Muffin Man 217

The Coachman. 217

The Miller of Dee 217

The Case of the Disgusting
  Doughnuts. 218

Mia's Star Surprise 220

Molly Mouse 222

Tiger. 222

Now the Day Is Over. 224

I Saw a Ship 225

Fairer Princess Sarah 226

Where Are You Going to,
  My Pretty Maid? 228

Monday's Child 229

The Case of the Ghost in the Attic . . . 230

Star Light, Star Bright. 232

Little Cottage. 232

Here Is the Church. 232

How Many Miles to Babylon? 233

A Swarm of Bees in May 233

Tinker, Tailor 233

Kylee in the Spotlight 234

The Midnight Fairies 236

Fudge Won't Play 240

Lost Billy 242

Pretty Polly 243

Here We Go Round the
  Mulberry Bush 244

Lavender's Blue 245

Itsy Bitsy Spider. 246

Bow, Wow, Wow. 246

The Cold Old House 246

Hickory, Dickory, Dock 247

Bat, Bat 247

Little Jack Horner 247

Twinkle the Tooth Fairy. 248

Rain, Rain, Go Away! 252

Too Much Sun. 253

The Case of the Stolen Necklace 254

Poor Peep 256

Fairy Seasons 258

My Mom Is Great 260

Happy Princess Haley. 262

Polly Put the Kettle On 264

I Scream 264

A Peanut 264

Our Baby. 265

Pat-a-Cake. 265

Dibbity, Dibbity, Dibbity, Doe 265

Like a Duck to Water 266

Maud and the Monster 267

Windy's Blowy Day. 268
Christmas Tree Fairy 269
The Magical Locket. 270
Sophie's Baby. 274
Ring-a-Ring o'Roses 276
See a Pin and Pick It Up 276
Miss Mary Mack 276
Mr Nobody 277
Little Sally Waters. 277
Georgie, Porgie. 277
Minnie and Winnie 278
Lady Moon. 279
The Case of the Crop Circles 280
Creatures 282
Queen of the Monsters. 283
The Little Turtle Dove 284
Hey, My Kitten 284
Dickery, Dickery, Dare 285
Clap Hands 285
Pussycat Ate the Dumplings. 285
Mrs. White. 285
Lucky Digger. 286
Magical Shoes 288
Dizzy Ballerina Izzy 292
Cats and Dogs 294
I Bought an Old Man 294
Hearts 294
New Hay. 295
Two Little Dogs 295
Mother Shuttle. 295
The Key of the Kingdom 296
Ten Green Bottles. 297
As I Was Going to St. Ives 298
I Saw Three Ships. 299

The Case of the Carnival Crasher 300
Black Beauty Grows Up 302
Little Husband. 306
The Robins. 306
The Merchants of London 306
The Dame of Dundee. 307
Christmas Eve 307
Gingerbread Men. 307
Egg Raiders 308
Mary Had a Little Lamb. 310
Song of the Stars 311
In the Tree Top 312
Mother Hubbard 313
Shy Ballerina Di 314
Little Kitten. 316
Cuddly Kittens. 317
Smoky the Dragon. 318
A Tiger for Tara 319
Man Overboard! 320
The Wedding 322
First 322
Gee Up, Neddy 322
Slowly, Slowly 323
Hark! Hark!. 323
The Little Bird 323
My Little Puppy. 324
Dolphin Finds a Star 328
What a Bad Goat! 330
Silly Pig 331
Beach Rescue 332
Sam Duckling Swims. 334
Lost in the Jungle. 335
What Do You Think? 336
The Baby in the Cradle 336

Contents

A Cat Came Fiddling 336

Bobby Shaftoe 337

Dance to Your Daddy 337

Teeth. 337

Black Beauty's New Owners 338

I Hear Thunder 342

Getting Dressed 343

Showy Ballerina Zoe 344

Tidal Pool Friends 346

The Flyaway Fairy 347

Stranded. 348

Polar Bear and the Rainbow 350

Give Me a Hug! 352

A Thorn 354

Cross Patch. 354

Baa, Baa, Black Sheep 354

Go to Bed Late. 355

Pussycat Mole 355

On the Grassy Banks. 355

Brave Little Deer 356

Kind Little Bear. 356

I Love You, Grandma. 358

My Little Kitten. 360

Lucky Little Duck 364

Shy Little Bunny 365

Pussycat, Pussycat. 366

Silly Sally. 366

Rock-a-bye, Baby 366

There Was an Old Woman 366

Frisky Lamb. 367

Frog Went a-Courtin'. 367

Little Lamb 368

Little Calf. 369

The Storm 370

Black Beauty Finds a Home 372

Bye Baby Bunting. 376

Hush-a-bye, Baby 376

A Star. 376

Nothing-at-all. 377

There Was an Old Woman Had Three
     Sons 377

Old Mother Goose 377

I Love You, Mommy. 378

Lost at Sea 380

Index 382

The Soccer Fairy

Georgina loved to play soccer. But there was just one problem.

"I'm fed up with these silly wings," she said one day after a game, wiggling her shoulders. "They just get in the way."

"Flying is great! And anyway, soccer is a game for elves, not fairies!" said her friend Sparkle.

"In that case, I don't want to be a fairy!" said Georgina, and stamped off.

"She'll change her mind," said Sparkle to herself. "Just wait and see."

The next time Georgina played soccer, the game was very rough. One elf kicked the ball so hard it flew high into a tree overhanging the field and hit a birds' nest—with an egg in it!

The egg tipped...teetered...and began to wobble, but none of the elves noticed. They were far too busy arguing with the referee about who had fouled whom.

Just in time, Georgina glanced up and saw the egg falling from the nest. She caught the egg before it hit the ground. Then she flew back up to the nest.

"Thank you," said the mommy bird, tucking the egg back under her. "But please, be more careful when you play soccer!"

The next time she played soccer,

Georgina checked the tree first. The mommy bird was away. "Good!" she thought. "She can't complain this time."

But, thanks to a naughty elf, the soccer ball knocked into the birds' nest once again. A small bundle of feathers tumbled out. It was a baby bird!

Georgina saw it and, quick as lightning, flew up to catch him. Gently, she held him in her arms and flew back to the nest. When he was safely inside, she sprinkled him with fairy dust to keep him from further harm.

Just then the mommy bird came back.

"I will tell everyone about your kindness," she said, when Georgina explained what had happened. "And, as you're such a good fairy, will you be baby Beak's godmother?"

"Oh, thank you! I'd be delighted!" said Georgina.

When they heard the news, the other fairies were very proud of her.

"Perhaps it's not so bad being a fairy after all," grinned Georgina, happily. "But I'm still going to play soccer!"

One Snowy Day

One snowy day, Old Bear poked his nose out of his den and saw the deep snow that had fallen while he was asleep.

"I'll take a stroll in the woods," he said. Off he went, his great paws padding along. How he loved the snow! He loved the way it crunched under his feet. Old Bear walked far into the woods, and forgot to look where he was going.

After a while, Old Bear stopped. "I'll just take a rest," he said to himself. "I'm not really sure where I am, but I can follow my pawprints home."

He closed his eyes and soon fell fast asleep. Meanwhile, the snow started to fall again...

By the time Old Bear woke up, his trail of paw prints had disappeared! "Now I'll never find my way home!" he groaned.

Then, he noticed an old tree stump nearby.

"That looks familiar. And so does that fallen log over there. If I'm not mistaken, I've walked in a big circle, and ended up at home!" he chuckled, turning toward his den. "What a clever old bear I am, after all!"

Elsie Elephant's Jungle Shower

There wasn't a cloud in the sky, and Elsie Elephant was feeling very hot.

"It's even hot in the shade," she grumbled. "I think I'll go to the river to cool off!"

Tommy Monkey was swinging high up in the tree tops. "I'm going swimming," Elsie told him. "You can come, too, if you like."

"You've got a very long trunk," said Tommy as they wandered toward the river. "What's it for?"

Elsie thought for a minute. "I'm not really sure," she said.

At the river they found Leo Lion standing at the edge of the water, looking in.

"Are you coming for a swim?" asked Elsie.

"Big cats don't swim," sighed Leo. "But I'm so hot!" He watched as Elsie and Tommy splashed into the river.

Elsie saw how hot Leo looked. She looked at her trunk—and had an idea! Filling her trunk with water, she sprayed it all over Leo.

"Thanks, Elsie. This is great!" said Leo.

"*Now* I know what my long trunk is for!" laughed Elsie.

There Was an Old Man from Peru

There was an old man from Peru
Who dreamed he was eating his shoe.
He woke in a fright
In the middle of the night
And found it was perfectly true.

I Eat My Peas with Honey

I eat my peas with honey,
I've done it all my life,
It makes the peas taste funny,
But it keeps them on my knife.

Haymaking

The maids in the meadow
Are making the hay,
The ducks in the river
Are swimming away.

The Old Woman's Three Cows

There was an old woman who had three cows,
Rosy and Colin and Dun.
Rosy and Colin were sold at the fair,
And Dun broke her heart in a fit of despair.
So there was an end of her three cows,
Rosy and Colin and Dun.

Sing, Sing

Sing, sing,
What should I sing?
The cat's run away
With the pudding string!
Do, do,
What shall I do?
The cat's run away
With the pudding too!

To the Snail

Snail, snail, put out
your horns,
And I will give you bread
and barley corns.

The Easter Bunny

The Easter Bunny's in a flap.
He'll never get it done!
Every year, it's just the same.
He's such a hot, cross bun!

He taps upon the henhouse door.
He hopes that they've been busy.
The hens laugh at his worried face.
He's always in a tizzy!

They fill his basket to the brim,
With eggs of every hue.
There's brown and white and speckled ones
And some are even blue!

The busy bunny hops and skips,
His way around the towns,
To make sure that the children wake
With smiles and not with frowns!

But what is this? There's one egg left.
He checks his list to see
If anyone has been left out.
"Oh, yes!" he smiles. "It's me!"

Bertha Saves the Day

Bertha Bunny had a shiny nose,
But this she could not mend,
Because her little powder puff
Was at the other end!

One day, the bunnies hopped and skipped
And wandered off to play
Too far into the Wicked Wood,
Then couldn't find their way!

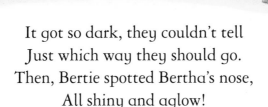

It got so dark, they couldn't tell
Just which way they should go.
Then, Bertie spotted Bertha's nose,
All shiny and aglow!

"Bertha's nose will light our way!"
Cried Bertie Bun, with gusto.
"Yippeeee!" the other bunnies yelled.
"We'll soon be in our burrows!"

Thank You, Kitty

"Kitty," called Cat one day. "I've got a surprise for you."

Kitty bounced over.

"You can have loads of fun with this ball of yarn," said Cat.

Soon Kitty was leaping around. "Watch me, Mom! I can pat the ball into the air," she shouted.

"Kitty," called Mother Bird. "Please may I have some yarn for my nest?"

Kitty looked at Cat. "I won't have anything to play with," she said sadly. "It won't be any fun."

Cat smiled. "It's much more fun to share things," she said.

Kitty and Cat watched the bird tuck the yarn into her nest.

"The baby birds like the yarn, don't they, Mom?" laughed Kitty. "I like sharing. Who else can I share my yarn with?"

"Why don't you ask the rabbits?" said Cat.

"We're having a hopping race," said Little Rabbit. "A piece of yarn is just what we need to make a finishing line. Thank you!"

Just then Cat called Kitty over. "I have a surprise for you," she said. "It's a bell from Mother Bird. To thank you for sharing your yarn."

"What a lovely present," said Kitty. "Would you like to play with it too, Mom?"

You Can Do It, Kitty

It was a lovely day. Kitty and Cat were having fun.

"Climbing trees is fun," said Cat. "Watch me, Kitty." Cat leaped up the tree.

"Climb up, Kitty," called Cat. "You'll love it up here."

Kitty ran to the tree. But then she started to cry. "I can't," she sobbed. "It's too high."

Cat jumped down and gave Kitty a snuggle. "Don't be upset," she said. "You can do anything you want to do. You'll soon be at the top of the tree. See that little calf over there, Kitty? He is trying to walk."

"But he can't even stand up," said Kitty.

"Keep watching," said Cat. "Now he can run and jump."

Kitty took a deep breath. "Watch me, Mom! I'm going to do it!" she said. Kitty ran to the tree and…jumped!

"It's great up here, Mom," shouted Kitty. "I can see the whole farm!"

The Princess and the Pea

A long time ago, in a land far away, there lived a king and queen who had just one son. The prince was grown up and it was time for him to marry a princess.

"And she must be a real princess," the prince told the king and queen.

But there were no princesses in the land where he lived, so the king and queen arranged for the prince to travel to strange and distant lands to find a bride.

The prince traveled north through frozen lands, until he came to a castle where a princess lived.

This princess was tall and fair and very clever. But she was also vain and boastful.

"A real princess would not be boastful," thought the prince. So he traveled south through hot, sandy deserts, until he came

to a palace where a princess lived.

This princess was very beautiful but was also very proud.

"A real princess would not be so proud," thought the prince. And he traveled east through misty lands, until he came to a mansion where a princess lived.

This princess had a charming smile and a lovely voice—but she told the most shocking lies!

"A real princess would never tell lies," thought the prince, so he returned home from his travels, weary, sad, and lonely.

One evening, not long after the prince had come home, a terrible storm blew in from the west.

Suddenly, there was a knock at the palace door! The king was so surprised that he went to answer it himself.

There, standing in the windy doorway, was the most bedraggled young woman the king had ever seen.

"Good evening, Your Majesty," she said to the king, curtseying politely. "I am a princess, and I need shelter for the night. May I please come in?"

"Of course," said the king. "We will gladly give you shelter for the night."

When the king told the prince that a princess had turned up at the door, the prince was very eager to meet her. But the queen told him he would have to wait.

"The princess said that she couldn't possibly meet you wet and bedraggled," the queen explained. "She has gone to have a bath and change into some dry clothes."

"That's a good sign," said the prince. "But how can we be

certain that she is a real princess?"

"I have an idea," said his mother. "Leave everything to me."

A short while later, the princess arrived in the main hall dressed in the queen's clothes. Her hair shone, her cheeks were rosy, and her eyes sparkled merrily to match her smile.

The prince and princess sat beside the fire and talked for hours. The prince was enchanted—but he still wasn't sure that the princess was a real princess.

Meanwhile, the queen went to the best guest bedroom carrying a single, tiny dried pea.

In the bedroom, she put the pea under the mattress. Then she asked a servant to bring another mattress to put on top of the first, and then another mattress, and another...until there were *twenty* mattresses on the bed!

Then the queen told the servant to put twenty soft, cozy quilts on top of the mattresses, and she had a ladder brought for the princess.

The princess was surprised when the queen brought her to the bedroom with its towering bed and ladder. But she didn't protest or complain. She thanked the queen and wished her good night.

The princess climbed the ladder to the very top of the bed. Sighing contentedly, she settled down to sleep. But the princess did not sleep a wink. She tossed and turned all night.

By morning, the princess felt tired and weary. When she came down to breakfast, the prince, the king, and the queen greeted her eagerly.

"Did you sleep well?" asked the queen.

"I'm afraid not," sighed the princess. "There was something small and hard in the bed, and no matter which way I turned, I still felt it. I'm dreadfully tired, for I hardly slept at all."

"I'm so sorry," said the queen. "But I'm delighted, too! For this proves that you are indeed a real princess! Only a real princess would feel a tiny pea under twenty mattresses and twenty quilts!"

The prince was overjoyed, for he had already fallen in love with the princess, and she had fallen in love with him. And so they were married.

And what happened to the pea? It was put on a velvet cushion in a glass case, and was sent to the museum, where it is still on display today!

Roses Are Red

Roses are red,
Violets are blue,
Sugar is sweet
And so are you.

Little Poll Parrot

Little Poll Parrot
Sat in his garret
Eating toast and tea;
A little brown mouse
Jumped into the house,
And stole it all away.

I Had a Little Horse

I had a little horse,
His name was Dappled Gray,
His head was made of gingerbread,
His tail was made of hay.
He could amble, he could trot,
He could carry the mustard pot,
He could amble, he could trot,
Through the old town of Windsor.

The Legacy

My father died a month ago
And left me all his riches;
A feather bed, a wooden leg,
And a pair of leather breeches;
A coffeepot without a spout,
And a cup without a handle,
A tobacco pipe without a lid,
And half a tiny candle.

Sowing Corn

One for the mouse
One for the crow,
One to rot,
One to grow.

Small Is the Wren

Small is the wren,
Black is the rook,
Great is the sinner
That steals this book.

Jalissa and the Jewels

Jalissa was the prettiest mermaid in the lagoon. Her jet-black hair reached right down to the tip of her swishy, fishy tail. Her eyes were as green as emeralds, and her skin was as white as the whitest pearl. And she knew it!

"That Jalissa thinks too much of herself!" the other mermaids would say. "One of these days she'll get into trouble."

Only one creature was fond of Jalissa. Gentle the giant turtle followed her wherever she went. But Jalissa didn't notice Gentle. She lived in her own world, spending all her time combing her hair and looking in the mirror.

One day Jalissa overheard the other mermaids talking about a pirate ship that had sunk to the bottom of the ocean. Onboard was a treasure chest filled with precious jewels. "But no one dares take the jewels," whispered the mermaids, "because the pirate ship is cursed!"

"I'm going to find that pirate ship," Jalissa thought. "Just imagine how beautiful I will look wearing all those jewels!" She set off right away.

Jalissa swam to a deep part of the ocean she had never been to before. She swam down until she found the shipwreck.

She saw the treasure chest through a porthole. Jalissa

swam inside and reached out to touch
the chest. The lid sprang open and
sparkling jewels spilled over the sides.

Jalissa lifted out a necklace and put
it around her neck. There was a little
gold and silver mirror in the chest. She
held it up to admire her reflection. It
was beautiful! Jalissa looked lovelier
than ever.

Suddenly, there was a loud crack
and the mirror shattered. The necklace turned to stone around
her neck—it was the ship's curse! Jalissa tried to swim, but the
necklace was so heavy she couldn't move.

"Help!" Jalissa cried out. "Help! Help!"

Gentle the giant turtle had followed Jalissa down to the
shipwreck. He heard her and swam to the porthole.

"Help me, Gentle," cried Jalissa, when she saw him. "Please
help me!"

Gentle's powerful flippers broke the necklace and freed
Jalissa. As they swam away from the wreck, Gentle said, "You
don't need fancy jewels, Jalissa. You're pretty
without them."

Once she was safely home, Jalissa
told the other mermaids that the story
about the curse was true.

"And I've learned my lesson," said
Jalissa. "I'll never be vain again."

Bella Bunny's Bonnet

In pretty Primrose Wood, there was great excitement. It was the Spring Parade. All the animals were joining in because prizes were being given for the best bonnets.

"I bet I'll win the prize for the prettiest bonnet," said Bella, who was a very vain bunny. "Now, what can I use to make it?"

She decided to gather some daffodils and harebells and weave them together.

At the parade Bella looked around at the other animals. "There isn't one hat as pretty as mine," she thought. "It looks good enough to eat!"

Unfortunately, Gordy the goat thought so, too. As he trotted behind Bella in the parade, he nibbled away at her bonnet until he had gobbled up nearly all the flowers!

Then Holly the horse gave a loud neigh. "And the winner of the prize for the funniest hat is...Bella Bunny!" she said.

Everyone cheered—except Bella. "But mine isn't funny, it's *beautiful*! Look!" she cried, taking the hat off her head—only to find that it was no more than a pile of twigs!

"Oops!" said Gordy. "Sorry, Bella."

Bella started to laugh. "I guess it serves me right for being so vain," she said. "And I suppose I did win a prize of some sort!"

Brave Billy Bunny

At the edge of Frog Pond Wood, lived a friendly little bunny called Billy and his little brother Bobby.

The one thing Billy really, really hated was getting wet! So one sunny day, when the other bunnies and Bobby hopped off to the stream to play, Billy ran through the wood, leaping over logs and weaving in and out of the trees. He was very fast!

Suddenly, he heard someone calling his name. It was Bouncer Bunny. "Billy! Come quickly!" he panted. "Bobby's fallen into the deep water and is being washed away!"

Billy rushed off toward the stream, leaving Bouncer far behind. When he reached it, he could just see Bobby in the distance, being quickly washed away downstream.

"Help!" cried Bobby. "I can't swim!"

Then Billy really began to run! He managed to get ahead of Bobby. He jumped into the water, swam up to his brother, and, coughing and spluttering, dragged Bobby to the side.

"Billy!" cried the others. "You're a hero!"

"A wet hero!" said Billy, grinning. "Getting wet wasn't so bad after all. I'm going for another swim—in shallow water!"

Kiana and the Butterfly

As Kiana Kitten lay dozing happily in the sun, something tickled her nose. She opened an eye and saw a butterfly fluttering just above her whiskers.

Kiana sprang after the butterfly, missed it, and landed in a bed of thistles.

"I'll catch that butterfly!" she said, crossly.

Kiana chased the butterfly toward the stream, where it settled on the branch of a tree. She climbed after it, but every time she came near, the butterfly simply flew away—and then she was stuck! She looked down at the stream swirling below her.

Just then, the butterfly fluttered past her nose. Without thinking, Kiana swiped at it with her paw. But as she did so, she lost her balance and went tumbling down through the tree, landing with a great *Splash!* in the water below.

"Help!" cried Kiana, waving her paws wildly. Luckily, she caught hold of a branch hanging over the stream and clambered onto the bank.

Kiana arrived home, cold and wet. She curled up, exhausted, in front of the fire, but just as she started to doze, she felt something tugging at her whiskers. She opened one eye and saw a little mouse.

"I've done enough chasing today, thank you!" said Kiana.

Home Sweet Home

Betty Bunny looked at the sweet green grass growing in the meadow on the far side of the stream. Her mommy had told her never to cross the stream, but she was tired of eating the rough grass that grew near her burrow.

"I'm going to cross the stream!" she said to her brothers and sisters, pointing to a fallen branch that lay across it.

Betty bounced safely across the branch and was soon eating the sweet, juicy grass on the other side of the stream.

"Come over the stream. It's lovely!" she said.

But just then, Betty's brothers and sisters saw a sly fox creeping up behind Betty through the grass!

"Look out!" they called.

Betty turned to see the fox just in time! She leaped back onto the branch, but she was in such a hurry that she slipped and fell into the stream. Luckily, friendly Becky Beaver had been watching and she pulled Betty safely to the other side.

"Home sweet home!" gasped Betty with relief. And she bounced off to join her brothers and sisters, vowing never to leave home again.

Rufus the Farm Kitten

Rufus the farm kitten liked nothing better than sleeping all day long, and all through the night. While all the other kittens were busy chasing mice or scaring away birds, he was normally fast asleep.

"Looks too much like hard work to me," he'd yawn, before strolling off to find a comfortable spot for a snooze.

One day, while the other kittens were chasing mice around the corn shed, Rufus stretched and looked around for somewhere to nap.

"You can't sleep here," said the farmer's wife, sweeping Rufus out of the kitchen. "Today's cleaning day and you'll just be in the way."

"You can't sleep here," mooed the cows, shooing him out of the milking shed. "We're busy being milked, and a kitten can never be trusted around milk."

"You can't sleep here," said the farmer, pushing him out of the dairy. "We're making ice cream and we don't want your hairs all over the place."

"I'm really tired," Rufus complained to a passing mouse. "Can I sleep with you mice?"

"Don't be ridiculous," laughed the mouse. "Don't you know that kittens are supposed to chase mice?"

Just as Rufus was about to give up hope of ever finding somewhere to sleep, he saw the ideal bed—a soft bale of hay sitting on a trailer.

"Purr-fect," he purred, curling into a Rufus ball. Within seconds, he was fast asleep.

He was so comfortable that he didn't wake up when the tractor pulling the trailer chugged into life. And he still didn't wake up when the tractor and trailer bumped down the road leading to town.

It was only when the trailer shuddered to a halt that Rufus woke with a start. He blinked his eyes, stretched, and jumped down. Then he blinked again. He couldn't believe his eyes! He was at a farmers' market—and the farmer had uncoupled the trailer and was driving away in the tractor.

"Wait for me," meowed Rufus, leaping down from the trailer. But the farmer had gone.

"I'll have to walk all the way home," thought Rufus.

Rufus walked all afternoon and all through the night. The rooster was just beginning to crow the morning in when he eventually made it back to the farm.

"Hello, lazybones," called the other kittens when they saw him. "Where have you been sleeping all night while we've been chasing mice?"

But for once Rufus really was tired—far too tired to explain where he had been all night. And it wasn't long before he was fast asleep!

A Hat Like That

Heather the cow took great care of her appearance. She had the shiniest hoofs and the glossiest coat. She had already won three rosettes at the County Show, and she wanted more.

One windy afternoon, when Heather was standing near a hedge, she found a beautiful straw hat on a branch. It had a couple of holes in it, but an elegant cow has to put her ears somewhere!

She strolled back across the field with her nose in the air and the hat placed firmly on her head. Heather couldn't wait to show it off to her friends.

But Desiree, Annabel, and Emily simply kept on munching. Heather tried a tiny ladylike cough.

The munching didn't stop for a second. So Heather coughed a little louder. The munching grew louder.

Heather couldn't bear it any longer. "Haven't you noticed it?" she mooed.

"Did I hear something?" asked Emily.

"It was me!" cried Heather, stamping her hoof crossly. "Look at my hat!"

Of course, the other cows had noticed the hat, but they loved to tease their friend.

"I always think,"

said Desiree, "that hats are a little...old-fashioned."

"Nonsense," Heather replied. "Only the most fashionable cows are wearing them."

"It's new then, is it?" asked Annabel.

"Certainly!" Heather replied. "It's the very latest style."

"Didn't Mrs. MacDonald have a hat like that a few years ago?" asked Emily.

"I don't think so!" Heather said firmly. "Mrs. MacDonald is lovely, but she's not what you would call stylish. Only a prize-winning cow could wear a hat like this."

"If you say so, dear," mooed Annabel.

That evening, the cows ambled into the farmyard to be milked.

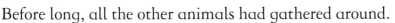

Before long, all the other animals had gathered around.

"They're admiring my hat!" whispered Heather to Desiree.

But the giggling and chuckling didn't sound as if they thought Heather looked beautiful. It sounded more like animals who thought she looked a little silly.

"Well, well! So that's what happened to Scarecrow Sam's hat!" cried Old MacDonald.

So nowadays, if Heather starts putting on airs and graces, Desiree, Emily, and Annabel know just what to do—they start talking about hats, and Heather tiptoes away.

Ariel's Song

Full fathom five thy father lies;
Of his bones are coral made;
Those are pearls that were his eyes:
Nothing of him that doth fade,
But doth suffer a sea change
Into something rich and strange:
Sea nymphs hourly ring his knell.
Ding-dong!
Hark! now I hear them,
Ding-dong, bell!

A Frog He Would a-Wooing Go

A frog he would a-wooing go,
Heigho! says Rowley,
Whether his mother would let him or no,
With a rowley, powley, gammon, and spinach.

A Candle

Little Nancy Etticoat
In a white petticoat,
And a red rose.
The longer she stands
The shorter she grows.

A Tisket, a Tasket

A tisket, a tasket,
A green and yellow basket.
I wrote a letter to my love,
And on the way I dropped it.
I dropped it, I dropped it,
And on the way I dropped it.
A little girl picked it up
And put it in her pocket.

My Black Hen

Tiggy-tiggy-touchwood, my black hen,
She lays eggs for gentlemen.
Sometimes nine and sometimes ten,
Tiggy-tiggy-touchwood, my black hen.

I Had a Little Hen

I had a little hen, the prettiest ever seen,
She washed me the dishes, and kept the house clean;
She went to the mill to fetch me some flour,
She brought it home in less than an hour;
She baked me my bread, she brewed me my ale,
She sat by the fire and told many a fine tale.

The Mischievous Mermaids

Of all the mermaids that lived in the sea, Jazz and Cassandra were the most mischievous. Their latest prank was to swim to the lighthouse, call out to the little boy, Jack, who lived there, and then dive under the waves before he could see them.

One day, Jack's mom had made him a picnic as a treat. Jack laid the food on a cloth on the rocks. He had leftover pizza and potato chips and soft drinks and chocolate.

The two mischievous mermaids popped up from the waves and saw all the food.

"Hi!" they called to Jack. "Are you going to eat all this food by yourself?"

Jack was very surprised. He'd never actually *seen* the mermaids before.

"Yes," said Jack. "I mean, no! You can have some of my picnic, if you like."

The mermaids had never had pizza, potato chips, soft drinks, or chocolate before. They ate so much they felt sick!

"Come back tomorrow!" called Jack, who was very excited to have met two *real* mermaids.

King Neptune was not happy when he found
out what Jazz and Cassandra had been
doing. "Mermaids cannot eat the food
that children eat!" he said.

"Humph!" said Cassandra. "I don't
believe a word of it. He just wants to
stop us from having any fun." So the
next day the two mischievous mermaids
swam up to the surface again to meet Jack.

The mermaids ate all Jack's food, then played
hide-and-seek in the waves, while Jack ran around the lighthouse
trying to find them. They came back the next day and the next.
But on the fourth day, when the mermaids said good-bye and
started to swim to the bottom of the sea, oh dear! Their tails had
become stiff and heavy and they couldn't swim anymore!

Jazz and Cassandra clung to the rocks and began to cry.

"What's wrong?" shouted Jack, alarmed.

When the mermaids explained they weren't supposed to eat
children's food, Jack knew exactly what to do! He got his net and
bucket and collected shrimp and seaweed from the tidal pools. For
three days and three nights he fed the mermaids mermaid food.
By the third day, they could move their tails again and swim.

When they arrived home King Neptune was waiting. But this
time, he wasn't angry—he was glad to see them back safely.

"I hope you two have learned a lesson," he said, gently.
"Jack has been a good friend, so you can play with him
again—as long as you don't eat his food!"

Two Princesses

Once upon a time there lived twin princesses called Charmina and Charlotte.

Although they were twins, they were opposites. Princess Charmina always curtseyed politely to the king and queen. And she remained really still while the dressmakers came to fit her new ball gown. Princess Charlotte was very different!

"Why do I have to dress like a powder puff?" grumbled Princess Charlotte when it was her turn to have a new ball gown fitted.

"How dare you speak to us like that!" her parents cried.

But she did dare. She dared to run barefoot through the gardens. She dared to wear her shabbiest clothes. In fact, she didn't behave like a princess at all!

One day there was to be a ball at the palace. The guests of honor were two princes from the next kingdom.

"Why don't you go for a walk until our guests arrive?" suggested the queen to the two princesses, who were already dressed. "But stay together, don't get dirty, and don't be late!"

The princesses walked to the end of the palace gardens. "Let's go into the forest," said Princess Charlotte.

"I don't think we should," said Princess Charmina. "Our gowns will get dirty." But Princess Charlotte had already set off.

They hadn't gone far when they heard a strange noise

coming from the next clearing.

"Let's turn back!" said Princess Charmina.

"It might be someone in distress!" said Princess Charlotte. "We have to check!"

They peeped around a tree into the clearing. In it were two horses, but there was no sign of their riders.

Then a voice called out, "Who's there?"

"Look!" said Princess Charmina. In the middle of the clearing there was a deep pit. The princesses crept up to it and peered over the edge. Princess Charmina stared in astonishment. Princess Charlotte burst out laughing. There at the bottom of the pit were the two princes.

"Well, don't just stand there," said the princes. "Get some rope from our saddlebags and help us out!"

The two princesses threw a rope down to the princes and tied the other end to the horses. Soon the princes were rescued.

Everyone enjoyed the ball that evening. The two princesses and two princes danced all night. And from that time on, Charlotte paid more attention to her gowns and hair, while Charmina became a little more playful and daring!

The Littlest Frog

Webster was the littlest frog on Mirror Pond, and every day he sat on his own, watching the other frogs play leapfrog over the water.

"Hop it, Webster!" they would croak. "You're far too small to join in our games."

"Please let me play with you," said Webster, one bright, moonlit night. "I can jump really high!"

The other frogs just laughed.

"But I can!" he insisted. He took a deep breath. "I can jump...over the moon!"

The other frogs laughed so much, they nearly fell off their lily pads.

"I'll prove it!" he said. "Just watch me."

One...two...three...*jump!* Webster leaped off his lily pad and sailed over the moon's reflection in the pond.

The other frogs stared in amazement. It was true. Webster could jump over the moon!

"We're sorry we didn't believe you," said one of the big frogs.

"Of course, you can play with us. You might not be the biggest frog on the pond, but you certainly are the smartest!"

Baby Bear's Friend

Baby Bear stretched and took a deep breath of fresh air. He was bursting with energy—all he needed was someone to play with.

"Come and play with me," he called to Owl.

"I only play at night!" said Owl, sleepily.

Nearby some little bunnies were playing. Baby Bear bounded over, but Mrs. Rabbit shooed him off. "Your paws will hurt my babies," she said. "You can't play with them."

Baby Bear wandered down to the river, where some beavers were hard at work building a dam.

"Come and play with me," called Baby Bear.

But the beavers were too busy gnawing wood. So he sat watching Kingfisher diving into the water.

"That looks like fun!" he said, jumping in with a splash!

"Go away!" said Kingfisher. "You'll disturb the fish!"

By now Baby Bear was feeling fed up and tired. He lay down and closed his eyes.

Just as Baby Bear was drifting off to sleep, a voice said, "Will you come and play with me?" He opened his eyes to see...another bear cub!

Baby Bear smiled. "I'm too tired to play now," he said. "But I'll play with you tomorrow!"

Don't Be Shy, Suzy

One day Suzy Kitten heard a lot of noise
coming from the farmyard.

"What is it, Mom?" she asked.

"There's a big game going on," said Mom.
"It looks fun, doesn't it, Suzy?"

Just then, Parsnip the pig saw Suzy. "Hello,
Suzy! Come and join in!" he said. But Suzy hid
behind Mom instead.

"What's the matter, Suzy?" asked Mom.

"The game is so loud. It makes me feel
shy," Suzy said sadly.

"There's no need to be shy," said Mom. "It's all your friends
playing the game."

But Suzy still felt shy. "I think I'll just watch," she said.

Then, Dennis the donkey gave the ball a big kick.

"Whoops!" said Dennis. "Did anyone see where the ball
went?" Quick as a flash, Suzy leaped up and raced up the tree.

"I can see the ball, Mom!" she shouted. "Here it is!"

Suzy threw it down from the tree.

"Thank you, Suzy!" the animals shouted.

The game started again and now Suzy was
right in the middle of things.

"Great kick, Suzy," shouted Parsnip.

"You were right, Mom," Suzy said.

"I didn't need to feel shy at all."

Suzy Helps Out

Suzy and Mom were going for a walk around the farm when Mom heard a noise.

"Someone's crying," she said. "What's the matter, Little Rabbit? Why are you crying?"

"I've lost my teddy bear," sniffed Little Rabbit. "It's my favorite toy."

"Don't worry," said Suzy. "We'll help you look for it. Perhaps it's behind the haystack."

"Well, I can't see Teddy," called Mom. "But here's your ball of yarn, Suzy!"

Suzy pointed to the gate. "Perhaps you left your teddy in the field, Little Rabbit," she said.

Little Rabbit began to cry again. "I'll never find my teddy."

"Don't give up," said Suzy kindly. "I'm sure we'll find it."

"Have you looked for your teddy at home, Little Rabbit?" asked Mom. "It could be there, you know. We've looked everywhere else."

So they walked slowly to Little Rabbit's home, carefully looking for Teddy on the way.

And, when they arrived, they found Teddy tucked right down inside Little Rabbit's bed!

Little Rabbit gave Suzy a big hug. "Thank you, Suzy and Mrs. Cat," he said. "I'd never have found my teddy without you!"

Oh, Bear!

There were posters all over town about the circus.

"I think I might join the circus," said Bear to his friend Rabbit.

"What would you do?" asked Rabbit.

"I'd walk the tightrope," said Bear. "It's so easy!"

He leaped onto the clothesline, gliding gracefully. He somersaulted superbly. He bowed beautifully. Then disaster struck! He wavered and wobbled. He teetered and tottered. He lost his grip and began to slip…

"Oh, Bear!" laughed Rabbit.

"Oh, well," said Bear, as he picked himself up. "Perhaps I'll ride a unicycle instead."

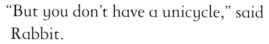

"But you don't have a unicycle," said Rabbit.

"I can fix that," said Bear. And he disappeared into his shed. Soon, Rabbit heard tools clanging and banging.

"There," called Bear, as he cycled out of the shed.

He pedaled up and down and pirouetted around and around. Then disaster struck!

"Oh, Bear!" laughed Rabbit.

"Oh, well," said Bear, as he picked himself up. "Perhaps I'll juggle instead."

"But there's nothing to juggle," said Rabbit.

"I'll find something," said Bear. And he disappeared into the kitchen. Rabbit waited patiently. He heard china clinking and clattering.

"There," said Bear, as he juggled down the path. He whirled the cups and twirled the plates. Higher and higher they went.

Then disaster struck! The cups and plates crashed down and the whole lot smashed.

"Oh, Bear!" laughed Rabbit. "I'm not sure the circus is a good idea."

"Nonsense!" said Bear. "Of course it is."

"But Bear," said Rabbit. "You've tried walking the tightrope. You've tried riding a unicycle. You've tried juggling. And look what happened."

"Yes," said Bear. "Look what happened. I made you laugh. Now I know exactly the right job for me." Quickly he ran indoors.

It wasn't long before he was back.

"Oh, Bear!" laughed Rabbit. "You're right. You make a perfect clown!"

Clumsy Fairy

Clumsy Corine was the worst in her dance class at Fairy School.

"Corine! Feathers, not elephants!" Madam Bouquet, the dance teacher, would say.

At the end of the year all the fairies were given a special task for the break.

"Corine," said Madam Bouquet, "your job is to paint this rose-petal lotion on a little girl called Alice's rash every night to make it better."

That night Corine flew in through Alice's window. So far so good! But then clumsy Corine knocked over a vase...

Alice woke up. "Who's there?" she asked sleepily.

"It's Corine," said the fairy. She explained why she had come. "You're not really supposed to see me," she added.

"Can you really do magic?" Alice asked Corine.

"Yes," Corine told her. "I'm good at magic. But I'm so clumsy!" She told Alice about her dance classes and Alice told Corine about her ballet lessons.

"I'll help you with your dancing if you like," Alice said to Corine.

By the end of the week, Alice's rash had gone, and Corine could pirouette.

Madam Bouquet couldn't believe her eyes. "Corine," she gasped, "what happened?"

Corine smiled. "It must be magic!" she said.

The Yellow Harebells

The fairies at Corner Cottage were always busy looking after the flowers in the yard.

It was Blossom's job to paint the harebells blue.

One evening, Blossom had a cold. "I don't think I can work tonight," she told her friend Petal, sniffing. "I'll have to ask the gnomes."

"No problem!" said Chip and Chuck when she asked them. "Just leave it to us."

When Blossom got up the next morning she was feeling much better—until she saw that the naughty gnomes had painted some of the harebells… *yellow*!

"Have you seen what they've done?" she said to Petal. "What will Jamie think?"

Jamie lived in Corner Cottage. That morning when he came out to play he noticed that something looked different.

"I'm sure those flowers were blue yesterday," he thought.

"Mom," he said, going into the kitchen, "I've picked you some flowers."

"Yellow harebells?" said Mom. "I don't remember planting those."

That night, Blossom painted all the harebells blue again. When Jamie and his mom went into the yard the next morning, everything was as it should be.

"It must have been fairies!" joked Mom.

Maria's Haircut

One spring day, Maria the sheep stood by the pond in Old MacDonald's farmyard, gazing sadly into the water.

"What is she doing?" whispered Doris the duck to her friend Dora. "You don't often see sheep near water."

Meanwhile, ducklings were swimming across to see who the visitor was.

"Sheep don't eat ducklings, do they?" asked Dora, anxiously.

"Of course not!" replied Doris.

Just then, Maria gave such a big sigh that she blew the ducklings right across the pond and they had to be rescued by their mothers!

"What's the trouble, my dear?" asked Old George, the horse. "Has your lamb run away again?"

"No," sighed Maria. "It isn't that. Just look at me!"

Old George looked carefully at Maria. "Well, you look even more, er, wonderfully woolly than usual," he said, gallantly.

50

"I look like a mess," said Maria. "My coat should have been trimmed weeks ago, but Old MacDonald seems to have forgotten."

"Hmmmm. He can be a little forgetful," said Old George. "I'll speak to the other animals and see what they suggest."

"Perhaps I could nibble her coat," said Percy the pig, who would eat almost anything!

"No, we need to remind Old MacDonald to give Maria a haircut," said Daisy the cow.

"Old MacDonald is always so busy," added Henrietta the hen. "How can we make him notice poor Maria's problem?"

That gave Daisy a very good idea. "It's Mrs. MacDonald

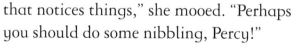

that notices things," she mooed. "Perhaps you should do some nibbling, Percy!"

So Percy did a little nibbling and the hens scurried away with the tufts of wool in their beaks, searching for the farmer.

When Old MacDonald went into the farmhouse for his lunch that day, Mrs. MacDonald threw up her hands in horror! "MacD!" she cried. "You're covered in wool! Don't bring all those fluffy bits into my clean kitchen! It's obviously time those sheep were shorn."

The very next day, Maria's haircut was the talk of the farmyard. And she and her friends strutted happily around, looking as smart and as stylish as any sheep you've ever seen.

Sunshine

A sunshiny shower
Won't last half an hour.

Mrs. Hen

Chook, chook, chook, chook, chook,
Good morning, Mrs. Hen.
How many chickens have you got?
Madam, I've got ten.
Four of them are yellow,
And four of them are brown,
And two of them are speckled red,
The nicest in the town.

Thaw

Over the land freckled with snow half thawed
The speculating rooks at their nests cawed,
And saw from elm tops, delicate as flower of grass,
What we below could not see, winter pass.

Little Boy Blue

Little Boy Blue, come blow your horn,
The sheep's in the meadow,
The cow's in the corn.
Where is the boy who looks after the sheep?
He's under a haycock fast asleep.
Will you wake him?
No, not I,
For if I do he's sure to cry.

Billy and Me

One, two, three,
I love coffee,
And Billy loves tea,
How good you be,
One two three,
I love coffee,
And Billy loves tea.

Little Nag

I had a little nag
That trotted up and down;
I bridled him, and saddled him,
And trotted out of town.

Sugarplum and the Butterfly

"Sugarplum," said the Fairy Queen, "I've got a very important job for you to do." Sugarplum was always given the most important work. The Fairy Queen said it was because she was the kindest and most helpful of all the fairies. "I want you to make a rose-petal ball gown for my birthday ball next week."

"It will be my pleasure," said Sugarplum happily.

Sugarplum began to gather cobwebs for the thread, and rose petals for the dress. While she was collecting the thread, she found a butterfly caught in a cobweb.

"Oh, you poor thing," sighed Sugarplum. Very carefully, she untangled the butterfly, but his wing was broken. Sugarplum laid the butterfly on a bed of feathers. She gathered some nectar from a special flower and fed him a drop at a time. Then she began to mend his wing with a magic spell.

After six days, the butterfly was better. He was very grateful. But now Sugarplum was behind with her work!

"Oh dear! I shall never finish the Fairy Queen's ball gown by tomorrow," she cried. "Whatever should I do?"

The butterfly comforted her. "Don't worry, Sugarplum," he

said. "We'll help you."

He gathered all his friends together.
There were yellow, blue, red, and
orange butterflies. He told them how
Sugarplum had rescued him from
the cobweb and helped to mend
his wing.

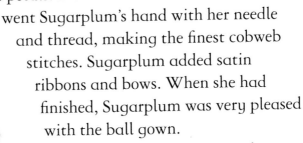

The butterflies gladly gathered
up loads of rose petals and dropped
them next to Sugarplum. Then the
butterflies flew away to gather more
cobwebs, while Sugarplum arranged all
the petals. Back and forth
went Sugarplum's hand with her needle
and thread, making the finest cobweb
stitches. Sugarplum added satin
ribbons and bows. When she had
finished, Sugarplum was very pleased
with the ball gown.

"Dear friend," she said to the
butterfly, "I couldn't have finished
the dress without your help."

"And I could never have flown
again without your kindness and
help," said the butterfly.

And the Fairy Queen was delighted
with her new ball gown!

The Elves and the Shoemaker

Once upon a time, there was a kind old shoemaker. He worked hard, but the day came when he had only a few pennies left, which was just enough to buy leather for one final pair of shoes.

That evening the shoemaker cut up the leather. Then, leaving it on his workbench, he climbed the stairs to bed.

The next morning the shoemaker couldn't believe his eyes. On his workbench was the finest pair of shoes he had ever seen. He put the shoes in his store window and that afternoon a fine gentleman bought them for a price that amazed the shoemaker.

The money was enough for him to buy enough leather to make two new pairs of shoes. The shoemaker cut up the leather and left it lying on his workbench. "I'll finish the shoes tomorrow," he yawned, and went to bed.

The next morning, when he came downstairs, the shoemaker saw two fine pairs of beautiful new shoes!

So it went on for weeks. Every night the shoemaker cut out the leather and left it on his workbench, and every morning there were splendid shoes waiting to be sold.

One night the shoemaker and his wife decided that they had to solve the mystery. So, after the shoemaker left the leather on his workbench, they shut up the store and hid in a closet.

When the clock struck midnight, two tiny elves appeared. They ran over to the workbench and began to stitch and sew, until they had made five pairs of shoes. Then they shot up the chimney.

"The elves must be frozen in those thin, tattered clothes," said the shoemaker. "And their feet are bare, although they make such beautiful shoes!"

So the shoemaker's wife made two little jackets and two pairs of pants. The shoemaker made two pairs of tiny boots, fastened with shiny silver buckles. The next evening, they wrapped the little clothes in tissue paper and left them on the workbench. Then they hid in the closet and waited.

At the stroke of midnight, the elves appeared. When they opened the presents, they were overjoyed. They put on their new clothes and danced happily all around the store, singing,

"See what handsome boys we are!
We will work on shoes no more!"

Then they flew up the chimney and were gone, never to return again! But the shoemaker and his wife never forgot them.

Kiss It Better

Rumpus was romping around the living room. He cartwheeled across the carpet. He turned a somersault on the couch.

"Be careful!" called Mom. Too late! Rumpus slipped from the couch, crumpled onto the carpet and banged his head on the floor.

"My head hurts!" he groaned.

"Come here and I'll kiss it better," said Mom. She hugged Rumpus and planted a kiss on his forehead. "Now, go and find something less rowdy to do," she said.

Rumpus rushed out into the yard and began to ride his bike. Around and around he raced.

"Watch out!" called Mom. Too late! Rumpus crashed into the corner of a bench, tumbled to the ground, and grazed his knee.

"My leg hurts!" he wailed.

"Come here and I'll kiss it better," said Mom. She planted a kiss on his knee.

"Now, find something safer to do," she said.

Rumpus ran up the grassy slope. Then he rolled down. "Head over heels, down the hill," he sang.

"Look where you're going!" called Mom. Too late! Rumpus rolled right into the rose bush. The thorns scratched him all along his arm.

"My arm's sore!" cried Rumpus.

"Come here and I'll kiss it better," said Mom, and she planted kisses all up his arm. "Now, try and keep out of trouble," she said.

Mom went into the kitchen. "I need a break," she thought. She made a cup of tea. Then, she sat down for five minutes. Just as she picked up her cup, Rumpus zoomed into the kitchen on his skateboard.

"Rumpus!" said Mom. She moved into the living room. She sat down and picked up the paper.

Boom! Boom! Boom! In marched Rumpus, banging on his drum. Mom sighed loudly.

"Is anything wrong?" asked Rumpus.

"I've got a headache!" said Mom.

"Never mind," smiled Rumpus, throwing his arms around her. "I'll soon kiss it better."

Helpful Baby Elephant

"Giraffe, you've lost your patterns in the mud," said Baby Elephant to his friend. "I'll spray you with my trunk."

"Monkey, you look very tired," said Baby Elephant to his friend. "I'll carry you on my back."

"Oh no, Rhino! You've fallen in the river," said Baby Elephant to his friend. "Hold onto my tail. I'll pull you out!"

Soon Baby Elephant needed a rest. He settled down under a tree and closed his eyes. But when he closed them, he noticed a lot of funny noises. Rustlings and warblings and the distant roar of lions. What if a lion was coming to eat him? Baby Elephant was scared! He opened his eyes with a start.

"What's the matter, Baby Elephant?" asked Monkey.

"When I close my eyes, I start to notice a lot of noises," explained Baby Elephant. "It makes me scared to go to sleep. What if a lion ate me while I was asleep?"

"Don't worry, Baby Elephant!" said Monkey. "Now it's our turn to help you. Settle down and close your eyes. Your friends will keep you as safe as safe can be while you rest."

"Thank you!" said Baby Elephant.

Sleepy Baby Tiger

Baby Tiger yawned as he followed Mom. It was so hot!

"Keep up!" said Mom to the tiger cubs. "Today, we are learning how to use our stripes as camouflage."

Baby Tiger wasn't too sure what camouflage was. And the long grass looked so soft and shady. When Mom wasn't looking, he stepped off the trail, curled up, and fell fast asleep.

Baby Tiger was woken a little while later by voices.

"He must be somewhere around here," said Mom's voice.

Baby Tiger felt very guilty. "Here I am," he called nervously.

"You were hiding!" said Mom.

"Camouflaged!" said one of the other cubs. "In the long grass."

"Er...yes," said Baby Tiger uncertainly.

Mom nuzzled Baby Tiger. "Don't hide for that long again," she said. "But that was wonderful camouflage. You used your stripes to hide yourself in the long grass like a grown-up tiger."

Baby Tiger smiled.

"Now follow me!" said Mom. "The next lesson is about how to stalk silently through the trees."

Maxine to the Rescue

Maxine was a very smart little poodle. Her hair was snowy white and fell in perfect curls. She wore a crisp red bow on top of her head. And she never went out without her sparkly jeweled collar.

But although Maxine was the smartest, most pampered pooch around, she was not happy. You see, she didn't have any doggy friends.

Whenever Madison her owner took Maxine walking in the park, Maxine tried her best to make friends, but the other dogs didn't want to be friendly with her. "Here comes Miss Snooty," they barked. Then they pointed and sniggered, before racing away.

And Maxine was never let off her velvet leash. "Those other dogs look tough," explained Madison. "You're far safer walking with me."

Maxine would have loved to run around with the other dogs. She thought that chasing sticks and balls looked like wonderful fun. And she was sure that she'd be able to swim in the lake if only Madison would let her.

But the other dogs didn't know that Maxine wanted to be one of them. They just took one look at her snowy white curls and sparkly collar and thought that she was too pampered for them.

"She doesn't want to get her paws dirty," Mrs. Collie

explained to Skip, her youngest pup, when he asked why
Maxine was always on a leash.

One day, Maxine was walking with
Madison in the park when she saw Skip
chasing ducks beside the lake.

"Careful!" barked Maxine, as Skip
bounced up and down excitedly. But
Skip was far too busy to listen. Then
Skip took an extra large bounce... into
the lake!

"Help, help!" barked Skip, as he
splashed about wildly in the lake. Maxine
gave a loud bark, and then, using all her strength, pulled the
leash from Madison's hand.

Maxine jumped in with a splash. Madison looked on in
horror as Maxine pulled the struggling pup ashore.

Once on dry land, Maxine gave herself a big shake, then
started to lick Skip dry.

"You were so brave, Maxine!"
cried Madison.

"Will you play with me?"
barked Skip, wagging his tail
hopefully.

After that, Madison always let
Maxine play with the other dogs
in the park, and Maxine was the
happiest little poodle around.

Hurt No Living Thing

Hurt no living thing:
Ladybug, nor butterfly,
Nor moth with dusty wing,
Nor cricket chirping cheerily,
Nor grasshopper so light of leap,
Nor dancing gnat, nor beetle fat,
Nor harmless worms that creep.

The Great Brown Owl

The brown owl sits in the ivy bush,
And she looketh wondrous wise,
With a horny beak beneath her cowl,
And a pair of large, round eyes.

She sat all day on the selfsame spray,
From sunrise till sunset;
And the dim gray light, it was all too bright
For the owl to see in yet.

"Jenny Owlet, Jenny Owlet," said a merry little bird,
"They say you're wondrous wise;
But I don't think you see, though you're looking at me
With your large, round, shining eyes."

But night came soon, and the pale white moon
Rolled high up in the skies;
And the great brown owl flew away in her cowl,
With her large, round, shining eyes.

Mousie

Mousie comes a-creeping, creeping.
Mousie comes a-peeping, peeping.
Mousie says, "I'd like to stay, but I haven't time today."
Mousie pops into his hole
And says, "*Achoo!* I've caught a cold!"

Mrs. Mason's Basin

Mrs. Mason bought a basin,
Mrs. Tyson said, "What a nice one,"
"What did it cost?" asked Mrs. Frost,
"Half a dollar," said Mrs. Collar,
"Did it indeed," said Mrs. Reed,
"It did for certain," said Mrs. Burton.
Then Mrs. Nix, up to her tricks,
Threw the basin on the bricks.

Ride a Cock Horse

Ride a cock horse to Banbury Cross,
To see a fine lady ride on a white horse,
Rings on her fingers and bells on her toes,
She shall have music wherever she goes.

Grandma's Glasses

These are Grandma's glasses,
This is Grandma's hat;
Grandma claps her hands like this,
And rests them in her lap.

These are Grandpa's glasses,
This is Grandpa's hat;
Grandpa folds his arms like this,
And has a little nap.

Tickly, Tickly

Tickly, tickly, on your knee,
If you laugh, you don't love me.

Build a House with Five Bricks

Build a house with five bricks,
One, two, three, four, five.
Put a roof on top,
And a chimney, too,
Where the wind blows through!

Little Red Riding Hood

There was once a little girl who lived with her mother at the edge of a forest. She was kind and sweet, and everyone loved her. The little girl often wore a red velvet cape with a hood. So everyone called her Little Red Riding Hood.

One day, Little Red Riding Hood's mother put some cake and fruit in a basket.

"This is for Grandma," Mother told Little Red Riding Hood. "She isn't feeling well, and these goodies will cheer her up."

"Can I take the goodies to her?" asked Little Red Riding Hood. Her grandma lived on the other side of the forest.

"Of course," said Mother. "But you must promise to be very careful. Stay on the path, and don't speak to *any* strangers!"

"I promise, Mother," said Little Red Riding Hood, and off she went.

As Little Red Riding Hood skipped along the path through the forest, she didn't know that a sly, greedy old wolf was watching her!

A little way down the path, the wolf sprang out in front of her.

"Good morning, my dear!" said the wolf, with a big, toothy grin.

Little Red Riding Hood remembered

what her mother had told her, and she didn't speak to the wolf. She kept walking. But that sly old wolf just followed her!

"Where are you going on this fine morning?" the wolf asked.

Not wanting to be rude, Little Red Riding Hood answered, "To my grandma's house, on the other side of the forest, sir. She isn't feeling well, and I'm taking some goodies to cheer her up."

"Hmm," the wolf thought to himself. "This little girl might make a sweet snack, but her grandma would make a tasty meal!" He began to work out a crafty plan.

"Wouldn't your grandma like some pretty flowers?" the wolf asked Little Red Riding Hood.

"Yes, grandma loves flowers," said Little Red Riding Hood, and she began to gather flowers. She strayed farther and farther into the forest, forgetting her mother's warning.

Meanwhile, the wolf hurried straight to Grandma's house. He knocked on the door.

"Who's there?" called Grandma.

"It's Little Red Riding Hood," called the wolf, in his softest, sweetest voice.

"Just open the door and come in," said Grandma.

So the wolf opened the door and went right in.

Before poor Grandma knew what had happened, the wolf had gobbled her up in one big gulp.

Then the wolf put on Grandma's

nightcap and crept into her bed.

Soon, Little Red Riding Hood arrived at the cottage with a posy of flowers. She knocked on the door.

"Who's there?" called the wolf in his gentlest grandma voice.

"It's Little Red Riding Hood."

"Just open the door and come in," said the wolf.

So Little Red Riding Hood opened the door and went right in.

Little Red Riding Hood looked over at the bed.

"Poor Grandma must be very ill," she thought. "She looks so strange!" Little Red Riding Hood stepped closer to the bed.

"Oh, Grandma!" she gasped. "What big eyes you have!"

"All the better to see you with, my dear," said the wolf.

"Oh, Grandma!" she said. "What big ears you have!"

"All the better to hear you with, my dear," said the wolf.

"Oh, Grandma, what big hands you have!"

"All the better to hold you with!" said the wolf.

"Oh, Grandma!" she said. "What big teeth you have!"

"All the better to eat you with!" growled the wolf, jumping out of bed. And he gobbled up Little Red Riding Hood in one big gulp!

With his belly so full it was almost ready to burst, the wolf lay back down on the bed and fell fast asleep.

At that moment, a hunter was passing Grandma's house, and he heard a strange sound coming through the open window.

"The poor old woman is snoring very loudly!" the hunter said to himself. "I'd better go in and see if she's all right."

So, in went the hunter. Of course, he saw that it wasn't Grandma who was snoring at all—it was the wolf!

"I have been hunting you for a long time," he cried. "Now, at last, I have found you!" He raised his gun to shoot the wolf. But then he looked at the wolf's belly.

"You sly old wolf!" cried the hunter. "From the size of your belly, I'd say you've swallowed poor old Grandma!"

He took out his hunting knife and very carefully slit open the wolf's belly—zip, zip!

Out jumped Grandma—and Little Red Riding Hood, too!

"Thank you for saving us!" said Grandma.

While the wolf was still asleep, Little Red Riding Hood went outside and got some stones. She brought them in and filled the wolf's belly with them. Then the hunter stitched up the wolf's stomach as good as new.

When the wolf woke up a little while later, he had such a stomachache that he ran out of the house moaning and groaning. He went off to hide in a cave, and was never, ever seen again!

Two Little Kittens

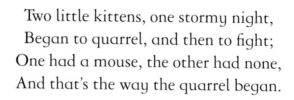

Two little kittens, one stormy night,
Began to quarrel, and then to fight;
One had a mouse, the other had none,
And that's the way the quarrel began.

"I'll have that mouse," said the biggest cat;
"You'll have that mouse? We'll see about that!"
"I will have that mouse," said the eldest son;
"You won't have the mouse," said the little one.

I told you before 'twas a stormy night
When these two little kittens began to fight.
The old woman seized her sweeping broom,
And swept the kittens right out of the room.

The ground was covered with frost and snow,
And the two little kittens had nowhere to go.
So they laid them down on the mat at the door,
While the old woman finished sweeping the floor.

Then they crept in, as quiet as mice,
All wet with snow, and cold as ice,
For they found it was better, that stormy night,
To lie down and sleep than to quarrel and fight.

Princess Sleepyhead

Good night, Princess Sleepyhead!
It's time to climb the stairs to bed.
Pick up your room. It's a mess!
Neatly hang your pretty dress.

Brush your teeth. Make sure they're clean.
Brush up and down until they gleam!
Put your jewels in their box.
Brush your long and silky locks.

Snuggle down, switch on your light.
It shines just like the stars at night.
Sleep tight beneath its cozy beams—
Good night, Princess. Have sweet dreams!

Slow Down, Max

On Old MacDonald's farm, no one works harder
than Max the farm dog—except, of course,
Old MacDonald! All day long, Max dashes
around the farm, keeping an eye on
everything that goes on. So, when Max
stayed in his doghouse one morning
with his head on his paws, everyone
began to worry.

"It's not like him at all," clucked Henrietta
the hen.

"He can hardly open his eyes," purred Milly the cat.

"I've never known him have a day's illness in his life," said
Old George the horse, "and I remember him as a pup."

Old MacDonald was more worried than any of them.

"Just stay there, old boy," he said gently. "I'll get someone
to help you." And he hurried off to call the vet.

The vet arrived very quickly. She, too, was very fond of Max.

She carefully examined him, lifting his paws one by one,
and checking every part of him thoroughly. Then she patted

the old dog's head and said, "You're like your master. You need to stop dashing around so much and take better care of yourself. You'll be fine in a day or two, but just slow down, Max. Take it easy for once, please."

Max nodded his head gratefully and went back to sleep.

Now, Mrs. MacDonald had been listening, and returned to the farmhouse with a thoughtful look on her face.

Max did as he was told, and by the end of the week he was okay again—it would soon be time to go back to work.

When he saw Old MacDonald rushing through the yard, hurrying to finish a job, Max dashed after him.

But Mrs. MacDonald rushed out of the farmhouse and called to the farmer.

"Husband!" she cried. "Did you hear what the vet said about Max? You must set him a good example! Please be a little more thoughtful!"

So, Old MacDonald began to slow down, and so did Max. The dog soon felt better for it—and so did Old MacDonald.

And Mrs. MacDonald, who had been begging her husband to take it easy for years, felt very happy indeed.

Jacob, the Shyest Rabbit

Jacob the rabbit was the shyest animal in the
glade beside Mirror Pond. He was too shy to
talk to anyone... too shy to play with the
other animals... too shy even to look out
from behind his big floppy ears.

"There's no need to be scared," Mamma
Rabbit told him. "If you want to join in, all
you have to do is ask."

But Jacob just hid behind the long grass. No one
even noticed that he was there!

One morning, Jacob was sitting beside Mirror Pond—alone,
as usual.

"I wish I could make a friend," he sighed. "But how can I,

when no one even notices me?"

Jacob gazed down sadly at the pond. He could hardly believe his eyes! There in the water was another little rabbit with big floppy ears, staring back at him.

"He looks just as scared as me!" thought Jacob.

He waved shyly at the rabbit in the water. The water rabbit waved, too! Jacob did a bunny hop in surprise. The water rabbit did a bunny hop.

"Hi!" said Jacob bravely, smiling.

"Hi!" said the rabbit, smiling back.

"So that's how you make friends!" cried Jacob, in amazement. "You just need to be a little bit brave and say 'Hi' to them."

He was so excited, he forgot all about being shy or scared. Instead, he raced off to tell everyone the good news.

And this time, everyone noticed him! Soon Jacob had loads of new friends to play with. But he never forgot to visit his very first friend in Mirror Pond!

Small and Pink

One morning, Percy the pig strutted proudly through the farmyard.

"Today's the day," he told everyone he passed.

"What is he going on about?" asked Doris the duck.

"Percy is expecting some piglets," clucked Jenny the hen.

"I didn't think boy pigs could have babies," said Doris, looking puzzled.

"No, no," Jenny clucked, flapping her wings. "They are coming from another farm to live here as part of his family."

Percy had tripped and trotted from one end of the farmyard to the other more times than he cared to remember, but Farmer Brown still hadn't returned with the new arrivals.

Percy went back to his pigpen and checked it one more time. It was spotless. The straw was piled up neatly along one wall and the water trough was clean and full.

"I must make sure that everything is ready for my piglets," said Percy, brushing a speck of dust from the doorway.

Just as Percy finished cleaning, brushing and tidying he heard Farmer Brown's truck rumbling into the farmyard. They were here at last!

Percy was so excited! He hurried from his pigpen, but before he could reach the truck…

Whoosh! Something very small, very pink, and very fast shot past his nose.

Whizzz! Something just as small and pink and even faster

scuttled under his tail.

Wheeeee! Another small and pink and noisy thing zoomed straight under Percy's belly.

"*Eeeeeeeeee!*" shrieked seven little piglets, dashing in every direction around the farmyard.

Late that night, a very tired Percy stood at the doorway of his pigpen—it was a mess. The straw was everywhere and the water trough was upside down. But seven little piglets were fast asleep in the corner.

"They never stand still, do they?" said Jasmine the sheep.

"No," sighed Percy.

"Are you having second thoughts, Percy?" asked Old Harry the horse.

But Percy gave the kind of grin that only a very happy and contented proud pig can give. "*Shhhhhhh!*" he whispered. "My babies are sleeping!"

The Emperor's New Clothes

Once upon a time, there was an emperor who loved new clothes. Every morning, the emperor swept through the palace in brand-new clothes, enjoying the admiration of everyone he met.

One day, the emperor told the chief minister to organize a grand parade.

"It will be a wonderful opportunity to show off a splendid new outfit!" said the emperor. "Find me the very best tailors and the very finest cloth in the kingdom!"

"Yes, Your Majesty," said the chief minister dutifully. He sent messengers to every corner of the land.

Two rascals heard the message about the emperor's parade. They hatched a daring plan.

A line of tailors soon appeared at the palace doors, with magnificent rolls of rich fabrics. But at the head of the line stood two tailors who seemed to have nothing at all.

"We have something very special to show the emperor," said the two tailors. "Something no one has ever seen before."

Impressed, the chief minister ushered them into the palace. The tailors stood before the emperor, holding out their arms.

"This, Your Majesty," said the first man, "is the most amazing cloth in the whole world."

"It is invisible," said his companion, "but only to fools and simpletons. Anyone with wisdom can see how beautiful it is."

Of course, the emperor could not see anything—because there was nothing there! The tailors were actually the two daring cheats, who had come to trick him.

Not wanting to look like a fool, the emperor said, "Yes, this cloth is magnificent." He immediately ordered a new outfit made of the splendid cloth. A workshop was set up for the two daring rascals. They asked for payment in advance, so the emperor gave them a purse filled with coins.

"We will need a loom and the finest gold thread in the kingdom," they told the emperor.

When the loom and thread arrived, the two tailors set to work. Hiding the gold thread in their knapsacks, they began to "weave." But of course, the loom was empty!

The next day, the two tailors came to measure the emperor for his new outfit. One busied himself with the tape measure, while the other spoke to the chief minister.

"We will need more cloth than we thought," said the first tailor. "We must have more money and more gold thread."

"Of course," said the chief minister, handing over another bulging purse.

For the next few days and nights, the two rascals stayed in their workshop, with the doors locked.

As the day of the parade drew near, the emperor grew anxious. He told his chief minister to check on the tailors.

The two daring rascals refused to let the chief minister in.

"It will ruin the surprise," they told him. "But if you give us more money, we can finish the suit sooner."

The chief minister handed over another purse filled with coins, then went back to the emperor.

"The new suit is beautiful," he told the emperor.

The day of the parade arrived, and the tailors were summoned. As the emperor undressed, the tailors pretended to hand him his new clothes. And the emperor carefully pretended to put them on.

As the emperor strode proudly through the palace corridors, the palace courtiers and servants bowed and murmured words of praise. They all knew that the clothes were only invisible to fools and simpletons, and no one wanted to be thought a fool!

A huge crowd gathered to watch the grand parade.

Everyone wanted to know if their friends and neighbors were simple fools who couldn't see the emperor's new clothes.

At last the royal procession came into view. A fanfare of trumpets announced that the emperor was coming.

A gasp rose from the crowd, quickly followed by cheers.

"Look at the emperor's beautiful new clothes!" people cried.

At the back of the crowd, one little boy hopped up and down to see the emperor's magnificent new clothes. He pushed his way to the front of the crowd.

"The emperor has no clothes on!" he cried, pointing and laughing. The crowd fell silent. Then someone called out, "The boy is right! It's true—the emperor has no clothes on!"

Soon everyone in the crowd was saying it: "The emperor has no clothes on!" "The emperor has no clothes on!"

The emperor knew that they were right. He blushed with embarrassment. "I didn't want anyone to think I was a fool," he thought, "but I have turned out to be the biggest fool of all."

And so the emperor just kept walking, staring straight ahead. He didn't see the two daring rascals sneak away, laughing and clutching their bags of gold.

Little Miss Muffet

Little Miss Muffet
Sat on a tuffet,
Eating her curds and whey;
There came a big spider,
Who sat down beside her,
And frightened Miss Muffet away.

Little Jumping Joan

Here am I, little jumping Joan.
When nobody's with me,
I'm always alone.

There Was a Little Girl

There was a little girl, and she had a little curl
Right in the middle of her forehead;
When she was good she was very, very good,
But when she was bad she was horrid.

Anna Maria

Anna Maria she sat on the fire;
The fire was too hot, she sat on the pot;
The pot was too round, she sat on the ground;
The ground was too flat, she sat on the cat;
The cat ran away with Maria on her back.

Round-eared Cap

A pretty little girl in a round-eared cap
I met in the streets the other day;
She gave me such a thump,
That my heart it went bump;
I thought I should have fainted away!
I thought I should have fainted away!

Goldy Locks, Goldy Locks

Goldy locks, goldy locks,
Wilt thou be mine?
Thou shall not wash dishes,
Nor yet feed the swine;

But sit on a cushion,
And sew a fine seam,
And feed upon strawberries,
Sugar and cream.

I Love My Puppy

I love my puppy because he wags his tail,
When he comes to meet me it wags without fail!
He barks and jumps when he wants to play,
He'd like to chase my bouncy ball all of the day.

He fetches me sticks to throw for him.
(If they fall into the pond, then he'll go for a swim!)
He scampers beside me when we walk in the park,
When he sees other dogs he just *loves* to bark.

But I love him most of all when the day is done,
And we snuggle up close after having fun.

I Love My Kitten

I love my kitten because of her purr,
She purrs so softly when I stroke her fur!
She loves to pounce upon a ball of yarn,
And to curl up on the hay in our old barn.

She washes her face by licking her paws,
She does *try* not to scratch me with her claws,
She peeps through the doorway to see if dinner's there,
And if it isn't, she meows to make me aware!

But I love her most of all when she just sits and purrs,
With her tail curled all around her.

I Love My Pony

I love my pony because he neighs hello to me,
When he gallops through the meadows he looks so free,
He lets me sponge him and brush his soft shiny mane,
He'll go for a ride in the sun, wind, or rain.

He jumps at the show and wins loads of rosettes.
(But we haven't won a first-place one yet.)
He's fun to be with when we go for long rides,
When he canters beautifully I'm filled with pride.

But I love him most of all when we stand very close,
And he nuzzles me with his velvet-soft nose.

I Love My Bunny

I love my bunny because he twitches his nose,
He twitches it especially when the wind blows!
When he runs in the garden his fluffy white tail
Bobs up and down as he follows a trail.

He nibbles carrots with his bright white teeth,
And digs holes in the lawn to see what's beneath.
(If Mom's watching when he does that, she usually shouts,
I don't really know what the problem's about.)

But I love him most of all when he sits on my lap,
And I stroke his big floppy ears and he has a nap.

The Ugly Duckling

One sunny summer day, a mother duck built her nest among the reeds near the moat of an old castle. There she laid her eggs, and there she sat, keeping them warm, day after day.

Finally, the eggs began to crack. *Peep! Peep!*

Out popped each fuzzy little duckling's head, one after another.

Then Mother Duck noticed that one last egg, the biggest one of all, had not yet hatched.

Days later, the biggest egg began to crack.

"*Honk! Honk!*" said the duckling. He was much bigger and scruffier than the other ducklings.

"He's not as pretty as my other babies," Mother Duck said to herself. "But I'll look after him, just the same."

The next morning, Mother Duck took all her babies for their first swimming lesson. They followed her into the water, one by one. They all swam beautifully—and the big, ugly duckling swam best of all!

The other ducks came to watch.

"Who's that scruffy creature?" squawked one.

"He's my youngest duckling," said Mother Duck. "See how well he swims!"

"But he's so big and so *ugly*!" quacked the other ducks, laughing.

That afternoon, Mother Duck took all her ducklings to the farmyard.

As soon as the farmyard animals saw the ugly duckling, they began to laugh and shout.

"Most of your ducklings are lovely," clucked the hen. "But look at that big, scruffy, *ugly* one!"

"He's too ugly for this farmyard!" cackled the goose.

The same thing happened the next day, and the day after that. The ducks on the pond and the animals in the farmyard all teased the ugly duckling. Even his own brothers and sisters made fun of him. The ugly duckling had no friends at all.

The ugly duckling was so sad and lonely that he decided to run away, out into the big, wide world.

Early one morning, before anyone else was awake, he ran away, through the reeds, past the pond and the farmyard and the castle walls, till he came to a marsh.

There he saw a flock of wild ducks dabbling in the water.

"What kind of bird are you?" they asked.

"I'm a duckling," the ugly duckling replied.

"No, you're not," said the biggest duck. "You're much too ugly! We don't want to have anything to do with you!" And they turned away, leaving him alone.

The ugly duckling spent two lonely days on the marsh, until a group of hunters came, scaring all the ducks away.

The frightened ugly duckling ran over fields and meadows. He wandered far and wide until he came to a lake where he could swim and find food. There were other ducks there, but when they saw how ugly he was, they kept far away from him.

The ugly duckling stayed on the lake all summer. Then the fall came, and the weather began to grow cold. All the other ducks began to fly south, where the weather was warmer. The ugly duckling shivered by himself in the tall grass beside the lake.

One evening, just before sunset, the ugly duckling looked up and saw a flock of big, beautiful birds above him. Their white feathers gleamed and they had long, graceful necks. They were flying south, just like the ducks.

The ugly duckling stretched his neck to watch them.

"I wish I could go with them," he thought.

Fall turned to winter, and the lake froze solid. The ugly duckling couldn't swim any longer. His feathers were caked with ice and snow, and he couldn't find any food.

Luckily, a farmer found the ugly duckling and took him home. The farmer's wife warmed the ugly duckling up by the stove, and the farmer's children tried to play with him. But they were loud and rough.

The ugly duckling was frightened. He flapped his wings and knocked over a milk bucket. The farmer's wife chased him out of the house.

Somehow, the ugly duckling found his way to a swamp, and there he managed to live for the rest of the long, hard winter.

When spring came, the ugly duckling found his wings had grown bigger and stronger. He flew across the fields to a lake. There, he saw the beautiful birds he had seen last fall.

"Hi!" they said.

The ugly duckling looked around. He couldn't believe they were talking to him!

"We are swans," explained one of the birds. "And so are you, and you are a very fine young swan indeed!"

The ugly duckling looked down at his reflection in the water. It was true—a handsome swan looked back at him!

The other swans made a circle around him and nuzzled him with their beaks. "Welcome," they said. "We would be happy to have you in our flock!"

The new young swan thought his heart would burst.

"I never dreamed I could be so happy," he thought, "when I was a little ugly duckling."

And, looking around at his new friends, he knew that he would be happy forever.

Hamster Sleepover

Hannah looked out of her bedroom window. There, at last, were her best friends coming up the path.

Ashley and Emma had sleeping bags under their arms. Deisha was holding a green duvet. They all saw her and waved.

"This is going to be the best sleepover party ever!" Hannah said. She jumped off her bed and ran down the stairs.

After a dinner of pizza and chocolate cake—everyone's favorite—the girls got ready for bed.

"Hannah has never wanted to go to bed this early before!" joked her mom.

As the four friends snuggled down for the night in Hannah's room, there was a loud scratching noise at the bedroom door.

"What's that?" asked Deisha.

They all heard a loud meow.

"It's Tiger!" said Hannah with a grin. Tiger was Hannah's cat. "I think she wants to come in and play!"

"Should I let her in?" asked Emma, getting up.

There was a sudden shout from Deisha. "No! Don't open the door!" she said. "Where's Lulu? She isn't in her cage!"

The girls all looked at the hamster cage in the corner of the room. Deisha was right. Hannah's hamster, Lulu, was missing.

"Oh no!" said Hannah. "We have to find her! Quick!"

The girls began a mad hunt for Lulu, while Tiger scratched at the bedroom door.

"Hang on, Tiger!" Ashley called. "You can't come in yet!"

Deisha searched under Hannah's bed. Ashley looked through the pile of sleeping bags. Emma checked behind the bookcase. There was no sign of Lulu.

Hannah opened a drawer. "Sometimes she likes to sleep in my socks," she said. But Lulu wasn't there either.

"Where can she be?" Hannah groaned.

Just then, Emma saw something. "Look!" she said.

The girls laughed. They had found Lulu at last, curled up fast asleep in one of Hannah's pink slippers.

"She's having her very own sleepover!" Hannah said.

Silly Millie Jarter

Silly Millie Jarter,
Who has lost a garter,
In a shower of rain.
The miller found it,
The miller ground it,
And the miller gave it
To Millie again.

The Broom Song

Here's a large one for the lady,
Here's a small one for the baby;
Come buy, my pretty lady,
Come buy o' me a broom.

Cock Crow

The cock's on the wood pile
Blowing his horn,
The bull's in the barn
A-threshing the corn.

Chairs to Mend

If I'd as much money as I could spend,
I never would cry, "Old chairs to mend.
Old chairs to mend! Old chairs to mend!"
I never would cry, "Old chairs to mend!"

Puss in the Pantry

Hie, hie, says Anthony,
Puss is in the pantry,
Gnawing, gnawing,
A mutton, mutton bone;
See how she tumbles it,
See how she mumbles it,
See how she tosses
The mutton, mutton bone.

My Maid Mary

My maid Mary,
She minds the dairy,
While I go a-hoeing and mowing each morn;
Merrily runs the reel,
And the little spinning wheel,
While I am singing and mowing my corn.

The Owl and the Pussycat

The Owl and the Pussycat went to sea
In a beautiful pea-green boat.
They took some honey, and plenty of money,
Wrapped up in a five-pound note.
The Owl looked up to the stars above,
And sang to a small guitar,
"O lovely Pussy! O Pussy my love
What a beautiful Pussy you are, you are!
What a beautiful Pussy you are!"

Ten in the Bed

There were ten in the bed and the little one said,
"Roll over! Roll over!"
So they all rolled over and one fell out.

There were nine in the bed and the little one said,
"Roll over! Roll over!"
So they all rolled over and one fell out.

There were eight in the bed and the little one said,
"Roll over! Roll over!"
So they all rolled over and one fell out.

There were seven in the bed and the little one said,
"Roll over! Roll over!"
So they all rolled over and one fell out.

Etc.

The Rainy Day

Rain! It splashed on the windows, gurgled down the drainpipes, and made puddles all over the yard. And Danny and Samantha were bored. Bored, bored, bored!

Out in the pigpen, Bessie and her piglets wallowed in a giant mud bath. It was such fun! There were squeals of delight.

On the pond, the ducks bobbed along looking pleased with themselves. Rain was just water off a duck's back!

Down by the bridge, the river was rising higher and higher. Eventually, it spilled over its banks and brown muddy water flowed across the road and under the farm gate.

Joe was busy fixing the tractor in the barn when he heard a shout from the road and saw Jack the mailman struggling through the water on his bike.

"Help, Joe! I'm stranded!" called Jack.

"Don't worry, Jack," Joe shouted back. "We'll get you across."

Joe put down his tools and climbed up into the tractor cab. He started the engine and reversed out of the barn.

Samantha and Danny came out of the house in their raincoats and ran down to the bridge with Rover the dog.

"Look," gasped Samantha. "The ducklings are swimming all over the yard. And Jack's trapped by the flood!"

Joe rumbled up in the tractor. "Get on the trailer," he shouted to the children. "I'll reverse it through the flood."

"Nice weather for ducks," puffed Jack, as he scrambled aboard. "Thanks, kids. Oh, no! There goes my hat!"

Rover barked wildly and jumped in after it.

"Come back, Rover," cried Samantha. "You'll be swept away!"

"No he won't, silly," said Danny. "Rover's a champion swimmer. Go fetch it, boy!"

Rover grabbed the mailman's hat in his mouth, and paddled back to the trailer. He dropped it and wagged his tail.

"Good old Rover!" shouted everyone. "Well done, boy!" Rover shook himself furiously, spraying them all with water.

Joe drove back to the yard and they all jumped off the trailer.

"Thank you, everyone," said Jack, picking up his hat. "Especially you, Rover. I'm very fond of this old hat."

"Come inside," called Mom. "You're all wet through. And what a lot of excitement for a wet Tuesday morning!"

"Brave dog," said Danny, giving Rover a pat.

Spring

Sound the flute!
Now it's mute!
Birds delight,
Day and night,
Nightingale,
In the dale,
Lark in sky,
Merrily,
Merrily merrily, to welcome in the year.

Little boy,
Full of joy;
Little girl,
Sweet and small;
Cock does crow,
So do you;
Merry voice,
Infant noise;
Merrily, merrily, to welcome in the year.

All the Bells Were Ringing

All the bells were ringing
And all the birds were singing,
When Molly sat down crying
For her broken doll:
Oh you silly Moll!
Sobbing and sighing
For a broken doll,
When all the bells are ringing
And all the birds are singing.

The Gossips

Miss One, Two, and Three
Could never agree,
While they gossiped around
So eagerly.

Engine, Engine

Engine, engine, number nine,
Sliding down Chicago line;
When she's polished she will shine,
Engine, engine, number nine.

Buff

I had a dog
Whose name was Buff,
I sent him for
A bag of snuff;
He broke the bag
And spilt the stuff,
And that was all
My penny's worth.

Puss at the Door

Who's that ringing at my doorbell?
A little pussycat that isn't very well.
Rub its little nose with a little mutton fat,
That's the best cure for a little pussycat.

Three Ghostesses

Three little ghostesses,
Sitting on postesses,
Eating buttered toastesses,
Greasing their fistesses,
Up to their wristesses.
Oh what beastesses
To make such feastesses!

Laundry Day

The old woman must stand
At the tub, tub, tub,
The dirty clothes to rub, rub, rub;
But when they are clean,
And fit to be seen,
She'll dress like a lady
And dance like a queen.

The Ant and the Grasshopper

Grasshopper was a lively, happy insect, who didn't have a care in the world. He spent the long summer days relaxing in the sunshine or bouncing and dancing through the grass.

"Why are you working so hard?" asked Grasshopper one day, when he saw Ant struggling to carry some grain on her back. "It's such a sunny day! Come and play!"

"I've got no time, Grasshopper," said Ant. "I have to take this grain back to my nest, so that my family and I have enough food when winter comes. Have you built your nest yet?"

"Nest?" laughed Grasshopper. "Who needs a nest when life in the great outdoors is so wonderful? And there's plenty of food—why should I worry?"

Day after day, Grasshopper played while Ant worked. Soon the trees began to lose their leaves and the days began to get shorter and cooler. But lazy Grasshopper hardly noticed. He was still too busy enjoying himself.

A few days later, it began to snow. Grasshopper suddenly found himself cold and all alone. He was hungry and there wasn't a crumb of food to be found anywhere!

"I know," said Grasshopper. "Ant will help me." So he set out

to look for Ant's nest. It was safe and warm beneath a rock.

Ant came out to see him. "What do you want?" she asked.

"Please, Ant," said Grasshopper, "have you any food to spare?"

Ant looked at him. "All summer long, while we worked hard to gather food and prepare our nest, what did you do?"

"I played and had fun, of course," said Grasshopper. "That's what summer is for!"

"Well, you were wrong, weren't you," said Ant. "If you play all summer, then you must go hungry all winter."

"Yes," said Grasshopper sadly, as a tiny tear fell from the corner of his eye. "I've learned my lesson now. I just hope it isn't too late!"

Ant's heart softened. "Okay, come on in," she said. "I'll find some food for you."

Grasshopper gratefully crawled into the warm nest, where Ant and her family shared their food with him.

By the time spring came around, Grasshopper was fat and fit and ready to start building a nest of his very own!

Amber and the Flowers

Every year on the farm, the animals had a competition. Everyone liked to join in the fun, and there was a prize for the winner. The prize could be for anything. One year, it was for growing the best purple vegetables.

This year the prize was for the best display of flowers, and it was Amber the goat's turn to judge the prize.

On the day of the competition, Amber came into the tent first. She looked very important as she was taken to the first display made by Baron the sheep.

"So I just choose which flowers I like best?" Amber asked.

"Yes, we walk along the table, and whichever display you think is best wins the prize. This is Baron's display. He's spent all morning getting it right," said Blink the pig.

"It's called 'Daisies and Dandelions,'" said Baron proudly. The flowers were white and yellow and looked very pretty in a blue mug. Amber looked at them carefully. She sniffed them. And then she ate them.

The others were so surprised that they couldn't speak! They just stared as Amber went to the next display,

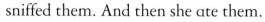

"Buttercups and Roses." She ate them too!

The goat tilted her head back, half-closed her eyes in a very thoughtful way, and compared "Buttercups and Roses" with "Daisies and Dandelions."

Moving along the line, she ate "Cowslips and Honeysuckle." Then she ate "Chrysanthemums and Poppies."

Amber wrinkled up her nose. "That one was a bit sour," she said. She turned at last and saw all the others looking at her with their mouths open.

"What?" she said, puzzled.

"What?" Rambo the bull said. "You were supposed to judge how pretty the flowers are!"

"Flowers are pretty as well as tasty?" asked Amber.

Everyone burst out laughing.

"Well," said Rambo, "I suppose it's another way of judging!"

So Baron won first prize...because Amber had decided that daisies and dandelions tasted the best!

At the end of the competition, the tradition was that the judge was given a bunch of flowers as a small thank-you gift.

Amber was very pleased with her gift... She ate it!

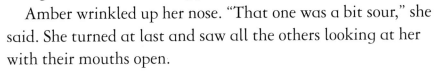

Hazel Squirrel

Hazel Squirrel had the finest tail of all the animals that lived beside Mirror Pond.

It was fluffier than Diana Duck's tail… bushier than Harvey Rabbit's tail…and swooshier than everybody's!

Each morning Hazel groomed her tail and admired her reflection in the pond. "I really do have a beautiful tail!" she would say, smiling at herself in the silvery water.

Sometimes Hazel played with her friends, but it usually resulted in tears.

"You splashed my lovely tail!" Hazel would shout crossly, when she played leapfrog with Webster.

"You're getting my tail dirty, Harvey!" she would moan

very grumpily, when they played digging.

Soon, Hazel stopped playing with her friends altogether. "I'm far too busy brushing my tail!" she said whenever they came to visit. "Come back some other time."

One morning, Hazel was admiring her tail by the pond as usual. Suddenly, she had a funny thought. She couldn't remember the last time she had seen her friends.

Hazel looked at her reflection in the pond. Staring back was a strange face…a cross face… a grumpy face. It was Hazel's face! Hazel couldn't believe her eyes. "No wonder my friends don't visit anymore," she cried. "I've forgotten how to smile!"

The next day Hazel called for her friends. They had such fun playing leapfrog and digging muddy holes that she forgot all about her tail. "From now on," she laughed, "the only time I'll look at my reflection is to practice smiling!"

The Dragon Who Was Scared of Flying

Once upon a time, in a land far away, there lived a dragon named Dennis who was scared of flying.

Every day his friends set off on adventures, leaving poor Dennis behind on his own. And every evening, the other dragons returned to their caves on the mountain with amazing tales of what they had been up to that day.

"I rescued a damsel in distress," one said.

"I fought the evil one-eyed giant and won," boasted another.

One day, Dennis could stand it no longer. Instead of retreating into his cave, he set off down the mountainside. It was very tiring having to walk.

Dennis was about to have a rest when he saw some brightly colored tents in the distance.

"I might take a closer look," thought Dennis. "Maybe I can have an adventure, too!"

When Dennis reached the tents he found himself in a world more exotic than he could ever have imagined. There were acrobats and tightrope walkers and trapeze artists, horses and clowns and a very fat ringmaster in a red coat. In such an incredible place, no one gave Dennis a second look. They just assumed he was part of the show!

The only person who knew for sure that Dennis wasn't part of the circus was Claude the ringmaster—because he owned it!

"Hi there!" he said. "Welcome to Claude's Circus. How do you do?"

"I'm Dennis the dragon," said Dennis.

"A dragon, eh?" said Claude. "Might be quite a crowd- puller! Would you like to join us?"

So Dennis joined the circus. Soon he was the circus's champion fire-eater. Folk came from far and near to see Dennis shooting flames high into the dark roof of the big top.

One evening, when Dennis had finished his act, he sat watching Carlotta, the tightrope walker, pirouetting high up on the rope as usual. All at once she lost her footing. Dennis saw to his horror that she was going to fall. Without thinking, he flapped his wings furiously—and found himself flying up toward her. He caught her and flew down to the ground. The crowd burst into applause. They obviously thought it was all part of the act.

"Thank you, Dennis," whispered Carlotta. "You saved my life."

Dennis was overjoyed. Not only had he saved Carlotta's life, he had also learned to fly. And, he said with a grin, "I do think that flying is a lot of fun."

Thank You

Thank you for your portrait,
I think it's very nice.
I've put it in the attic
To scare away the mice.

Cock Robin's Courtship

Cock Robin got up early
At the break of day,
And went to Jenny's window
To sing a roundelay.
He sang Cock Robin's love
To little Jenny Wren,
And when he got unto the end
Then he began again.

Grig's Pig

Grandpa Grig
Had a pig,
In a field of clover;
Piggy died,
Grandpa cried,
And all the fun was over.

Little Betty Blue

Little Betty Blue
Lost a lovely shoe,
What can little Betty do?
Give her another
To match the other,
And then she may
Swagger in two.

Seesaw, Margery Daw

Seesaw, Margery Daw,
Johnny shall have a new master;
He shall have but a penny a day,
Because he can't work any faster.

Elsie Marley

Elsie Marley's grown so fine,
She won't get up to feed the swine,
But lies in bed 'til eight or nine,
Lazy Elsie Marley!

The Swing

How do you like to go up in a swing,
Up in the air so blue?
Oh, I do think it the pleasantest thing
Ever a child can do!

Up in the air and over the wall,
'Til I can see so wide,
River and trees and cattle and all
Over the countryside—

'Til I look down on the garden green,
Down on the roof so brown—
Up in the air I go flying again,
Up in the air and down!

City Child

Dainty little maiden, whither would you wander?
Whither from this pretty home, the home where mother dwells?
"Far and far away," said the dainty little maiden,
"All among the gardens, auriculas, anemones,
Roses and lilies, and Canterbury bells."

Dainty little maiden, whither would you wander?
Whither from this pretty house, this city house of ours?
"Far and far away," said the dainty little maiden,
"All among the meadows, the clover, and the clematis,
Daisies and kingcups and honeysuckle flowers."

Copycat Max

Max was a little tiger with a bad habit. He copied everyone! When the parrot said, "Pretty Polly," Max repeated it. Then, when the parrot got angry and said, "Shut up, Max," he repeated that as well. It was very annoying.

One day, Max set off to annoy as many animals as possible.

Soon he met a brown chameleon sitting on a green leaf. The chameleon saw Max and changed his color to green.

"Watch this then," said Max, and he rolled over and over in some mud. "Now I'm brown," he said.

"You're not really brown," said the chameleon. "Only chameleons can change color."

"Hmmm!" said Max, annoyed. He rolled in some white feathers. They stuck to the mud. "Look," he said, "now I'm white!"

The chameleon started to laugh. "It won't last," he said.

When Max got home his mother was very angry with him for getting so dirty. She held Max down with her big paw and licked him until he was clean again. It took *ages*. Max wriggled and complained, but he couldn't get away.

"It serves you right for being such a copycat," said his mother. "I hope you've learned your lesson not to do it again."

"Oh, all right," said Max. And, for the moment, he meant it!

Forever Friends

Deisha Duckling had loads of friends but her best friend of all was Charlotte Cygnet. Every day they played together, chasing each other through the reeds.

"When I grow up, I'll be a beautiful swan like my mommy!" said Charlotte.

"And I'll be a dull brown duck," said Deisha. She worried that Charlotte would only want to play with her pretty swan friends when they grew up.

One day, the two were playing hide-and-seek when something dreadful happened. While Deisha hid among some large leaves, a sly fox crept up and snatched her in his mouth!

Before she had time to quack he was heading for his lair. But Charlotte had been watching. Without hesitating, she rushed after the fox and caught the tip of his long tail in her sharp beak. Then, as the fox spun around, she pecked him hard on the nose.

The fox's mouth dropped open and Deisha fell out. He slunk away.

Deisha couldn't thank her friend enough.

"That's what friends are for!" said Charlotte. "We'll always be friends."

And Mrs. Swan and Mrs. Duck, who were the best of friends, agreed.

My Grandpa Is Great

My grandpa is great. He always has plenty of time for me, even when he's busy.

I always look forward to going to stay with him for the weekend.

Grandpa is a lot like me. He enjoys getting really dirty. (I just wish Grandma felt the same way.)

My grandpa is a great fisherman, but he always forgets the size of the fish that he caught.

Luckily, I'm there to remind him!

Grandpa is a wonderful gardener. His pumpkins are the biggest I've ever seen.

(Well, that was until I saw some even bigger ones at the county show.)

Grandpa knows all about nature. When we go on a walk he knows the names of every bird and flower.

Grandpa is a fantastic dancer.

I love dancing with him, but sometimes it makes me feel a bit dizzy. I don't know where he gets his energy.

My grandpa is a great cook, too. He says that when I grow up, he'll tell me the secret of making the best pizza in the universe.

Grandpa tells me all kinds of amazing stories. It's hard to believe that he used to be a pirate! I wish I could have seen his big, red pirate ship.

Sometimes, if I'm really lucky, Grandpa lets me sleep in his tent.

When he's with me, I'm never afraid.

When it's time to go home, I wave good-bye to Grandpa.

I expect he's really busy when I'm not there to help him out with everything.

I really love going to Grandpa's because... my grandpa is *great*!

Snow White

One day, a queen gave birth to
a beautiful little girl, who had
skin as white as snow, cheeks as
red as blood, and hair as black
as ebony wood. She was called
Snow White.

Sadly, the queen soon died.
The king married again, and
the new queen was beautiful but
vain. Every day she stood before
her magic mirror and asked,
"Mirror, mirror, on the wall, who
is the fairest one of all?"

The mirror always said, "You, oh Queen, are fairest of all!"

But little Snow White grew more and more lovely. At last
the day came when the queen's magic mirror replied, "You, oh
Queen, are fair, it's true. But Snow White is fairer than you!"

The queen was very angry. She summoned her huntsman.

"Take Snow White into the forest and kill her," said the
wicked queen. "Bring me her heart in this chest."

So the huntsman took Snow White deep into the forest.
But when he looked at Snow White he could not do it.

The huntsman killed a wild pig, put its heart in the chest,
and returned to the castle. The wicked queen was pleased,
because she was sure that Snow White was dead.

Lost and alone, Snow White stumbled through the dark forest until she came to a little house. She knocked at the door, but there was no answer. The door was unlocked, so she walked in.

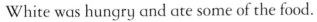

Inside, she saw a little table with seven little plates of food. Snow White was hungry and ate some of the food.

Soon, Snow White felt sleepy. She found seven cosy little beds. She lay down on one of them and fell fast asleep.

The house belonged to seven dwarfs who worked in the gold mines. When they returned home that night, they found Snow White. She told them her story. They felt sorry for her.

"If you cook and clean for us," they said, "you can stay here and we will look after you." So Snow White decided to stay.

At the castle, the wicked queen was looking in her magic mirror. This time the mirror said, "Snow White is as lovely as she is good. She lives with the dwarfs, deep in the wood!"

The queen was furious. She decided to kill Snow White herself. She made a magic potion and used it to poison a pretty hair comb. Then she set out for the dwarfs' house dressed as a poor peasant woman.

"Pretty combs to buy!" she cried.

Snow White went outside. The witch offered to comb Snow White's hair. When the poisoned comb touched Snow White's beautiful black hair, she fell to the floor as if she were dead.

That night, when the dwarfs came home, they found Snow White lying on the ground.

At first they were in despair, but then one of them noticed the comb. Very gently, the eldest dwarf took the comb out of Snow White's hair. Soon, her pale cheeks grew rosy again.

The next morning, when the dwarfs left for the mines, they made sure Snow White locked the door and they kept the key.

This time, when the queen's magic mirror told her that Snow White was still alive, she roared with fury.

The wicked queen made a magic potion. With the potion she poisoned one half of a rosy apple. Then she set off to the dwarfs' house dressed as an apple seller.

"Sweet, rosy apples to buy!" she called outside the window. But Snow White remembered the dwarfs' warning.

"I cannot let you in and I cannot come out," she said.

"Where is the harm in a sweet, rosy apple?" asked the apple-seller. "Look, I will take a bite from this side. It is so sweet and juicy! Taste it for yourself."

Snow White took the poisoned apple. The moment she bit the poisoned apple, she fell down, lifeless.

When the dwarfs found Snow White lying on the floor again, they did everything they could to try to wake her. But she was still and cold.

The dwarfs made a beautiful glass coffin for Snow White. They set it among the flowers in their garden.

One day, a prince came riding through the forest. When he saw Snow White, he instantly fell in love with her. He begged the dwarfs to let him take the casket to his palace.

When the dwarfs lifted the casket, they stumbled. Suddenly a piece of poisoned apple fell from Snow White's mouth and her eyes opened. Snow White was alive!

Of course, the moment Snow White set eyes on the prince, she fell in love with him. When he asked Snow White to marry him, she happily agreed.

The next time the wicked queen looked into her magic mirror, it said, "You, oh Queen, are fair, it is true. But there is one still fairer than you. The bride that the prince will marry tonight is none other than the lovely Snow White!"

The wicked queen was so enraged that she fell down dead. And Snow White had nothing to fear ever again.

Mary, Mary, Quite Contrary

Mary, Mary, quite contrary,
How does your garden grow?
With silver bells and cockle shells,
And pretty maids all in a row.

A Nickel

I went into my grandmother's garden,
And there I found a nickel.
I went into my next door neighbor's;
There I bought
A pipkin and a popkin,
A slipkin and a slopkin,
A nailboard, a sailboard,
And all for a nickel.

Here Comes a Widow

Here comes a widow from Barbary land,
With all her children in her hand;
One can brew, and one can bake,
And one can make a wedding cake.
Pray take one, pray take two,
Pray take one that pleases you.

Jack Sprat's Cat

Jack Sprat
Had a cat,
It had but one ear;
It went to buy butter
When butter was dear.

Butterfly

I'm a little butterfly
Born in a bower,
Christened in a teapot,
Died in half an hour.

An Egg

In marble halls as white as milk,
Lined with skin as soft as silk;
Within a fountain crystal clear,
A golden apple doth appear.
No doors there are to this stronghold—
Yet thieves break in and steal the gold.

Grumpy Fairy

Misery didn't have any friends. It was her own fault, she was always grumbling. Willow, her niece, couldn't understand

her. "Why do you always find fault with everyone?" she asked.

"Because everybody is so useless!" said her grumpy aunt.

One day Misery told the fairy who baked the bread, "Your bread is too soft. I like crusty bread."

"If that's your attitude," said the baker fairy, "bake your own bread!"

"I will!" said Misery.

The next day she was rude to the fairy who mended her shoes.

"No one speaks to me like that!" said the cobbler fairy. "From now on you can mend your own shoes."

"I'll be glad to," said Misery grumpily.

Then she insulted the fairy who collected honey from the bees.

"How dare you?" said the honey-collector fairy. "I'm not staying here to be insulted. You can collect your own honey."

"How are you going to manage?" Willow asked Misery.

"No problem," said Misery. "I'll do everything myself." And with that she set to work to bake some bread. Misery mixed and kneaded the dough and left it to rise. Then she put the loaf in the oven, and sat down for a well-earned rest. Soon she had

nodded off.

She was awoken by a smell of burning. All that was left of the loaf of bread were a few burned cinders. What Misery didn't realize was that the baker fairy used a special baking spell—a spell that Misery didn't know!

Misery went to collect some honey. She waved her arms at the bees buzzing around the hive, shouting, "Out of my way, bees." They didn't like it one little bit! Their answer was to swarm around her and sting her. What Misery didn't know was that the honey fairy used a special honey-collecting spell.

Misery ran from the bees as fast as she could. As she did, she broke her shoe! Oh dear! What a state she was in! Burned bread, bee stings, and only one shoe!

"You can't go on like this," said Willow, when she saw Misery.

Misery did some serious thinking. "Tell all the fairies I've turned over a new leaf," she told Willow. "From now on I won't be grumpy any more."

Willow was delighted! Misery didn't complain about anything for months after that, and Willow kept her fingers crossed that it would last.

The Little Doll

I once had a sweet little doll, dears,
The prettiest doll in the world;
Her cheeks were so red and white, dears,
And her hair was so charmingly curled.
But I lost my poor little doll, dears,
As I played on the hills one day;
And I cried for her more than a week, dears,
But I never could find where she lay.

I found my poor little doll, dears,
As I played on the hills one day;
Folks say she is terribly changed, dears,
For her paint is all washed away,
And her arms trodden off by the cows, dears,
And her hair not the least bit curled;
Yet for old sakes' sake, she is still, dears,
The prettiest doll in the world.

Skipping

Little children skip,
The rope so gaily gripping,
Tom and Harry,
Jane and Mary,
Kate, Diana,
Susan, Anna,
All are fond of skipping!

The little boats they skip,
Beside the heavy shipping,
And while the squalling
Winds are calling,
Falling, rising,
Rising, falling,
All are fond of skipping!

The dry fall leaves they skip,
When blasts the trees are stripping;
Bounding, whirling,
Sweeping, twirling,
And in wanton
Mazes curling,
All are fond of skipping!

Lion's Birthday

It was Lion's birthday.

"Hi, Elephant! Hi, Parrot!" said Lion.

"Er, hi!" trumpeted Elephant. They were both carrying bunches of flowers. "Sorry, Lion. We're kind of busy right now."

"Hi, Giraffe! Hi, Monkey!" said Lion. They were collecting coconuts from a tall palm tree.

"We're too busy to talk!" said Giraffe over his shoulder.

"Hi, Zebra! Hi, Hippo!" said Lion.

Zebra muttered something to Hippo. They disappeared behind a pineapple tree without even saying hi!

"The animals have all forgotten my birthday," said Lion, sadly. He walked slowly through the jungle, feeling very sad.

Then... *Happy birthday, Lion!* called all the animals.

"What a *surprise*!" roared Lion happily.

Sad Monkey

Tiny Monkey was sad, because he didn't know how to climb.

"All the other monkeys can climb," he thought.

"I'll teach you, Tiny Monkey," said Big Monkey, scampering up a tree. "Cling with your feet, and swing your tail—like this!"

"I'll lift you up into the tree to get you going," said Giraffe.

"I'll catch you if you fall down," said Lion.

"See if you can get all the way up to the top!" said Parrot, fluttering up to the topmost branch in a flash of color and then flying back down again.

Taking a deep breath, Tiny Monkey climbed onto Giraffe's neck. Her neck swayed as she lifted him high into the tree. Tiny Monkey took a deep breath and swung into the tree.

He clung with his feet and swung with his tail, just as Big Monkey had told him. And it worked! He scampered all the way to the top!

"Look at me! I'm the best climbing monkey in the forest!" he called.

Surprise Sleepover

It had been snowing all day. Hannah, Emma, and Deisha were at Ashley's house. Though it was still afternoon, it was growing dark already.

Suddenly the light in Ashley's room went out, and everything went very, very dark.

"What's happening?" yelled Hannah. The girls grabbed each other's hands in the dark.

"Let's go downstairs," said Ashley.

They stumbled forward and Ashley felt for the door handle. Finding it, she pulled the door open and the others followed her out onto the landing.

The light had gone out there, too. It was as black as night.

Ashley's mom came up the stairs holding a candle. "Don't panic, girls, it's just a blackout!" she said. "Come on, we'll make ourselves cozy in the sitting room."

Downstairs, Ashley's dad was building a fire in the hearth. "The snow's knocked out the power," he said. "And the roads are all blocked."

"But how will we get home?" Hannah asked.

Ashley's mom told them not to worry and went to call their parents.

Ashley's dad went to find some blankets. "Here, girls," he said. "These will keep you warm until the fire gets going."

The girls snuggled up on the two couches and watched as the fire began to crackle to life.

Ashley's mom came in a little later with some drinks. "I've got a bit of a surprise, girls!" she said. "Guess what?"

"What, Mom?" asked Ashley.

"You're all going to stay here tonight because of the snow!" she said with a smile. "You're having a surprise sleepover!"

"Yeah!" they all cheered.

"Snowstorms are great!" said Emma.

Minnie and Mattie

Minnie and Mattie
And fat little May,
Out in the country,
Spending a day.

Minnie and Mattie
And May carry posies,
Half of sweet violets,
Half of primroses.

Give the sun time enough,
Glowing and glowing,
He'll rouse the roses
And bring them blowing.

Don't wait for roses,
Losing today,
Oh Minnie, Mattie,
And wise little May.

Violets and primroses
Blossom today,
For Minnie and Mattie
And fat little May.

Meg Merrilees

Old Meg she was a gypsy,
And lived upon the moors:
Her bed it was the brown heath turf,
And her house was out of doors.

Her brothers were the craggy hills,
Her sisters larchen trees—
Alone with her great family
She lived as she did please.

No breakfast had she many a morn,
No dinner many a noon,
And 'stead of supper she would stare
Full hard against the moon.

Old Meg was brave as Margaret Queen,
And tall as Amazon:
An old red blanket cloak she wore;
A chip-hat had she on.
God rest her aged bones somewhere—
She died full long agone!

There Was an Old Woman Who Lived in a Shoe

There was an old woman who lived in a shoe,
She had so many children, she didn't know what to do;
She gave them some broth without any bread,
Then scolded them soundly and put them to bed.

There Was an Old Woman Tossed Up in a Basket

There was an old woman tossed up in a basket,
Nineteen times as high as the moon;
Where she was going I couldn't but ask it,
For in her hand she carried a broom.

"Old woman, old woman, old woman," quoth I,
"Oh whither, Oh whither, Oh whither, so high?"
"To brush the cobwebs off the sky!"
"Should I go with thee?" "Aye, by and by."

My Grandma Is Great

My grandma is great.

She's gentle, kind, and loads of fun. Sometimes when Mom and Dad go out for the evening, I go to Grandma's house to sleep. I always have a fantastic time because my grandma makes me feel special.

Grandma always knows exactly what I like to eat. She gives me the most delicious food.

(That's our little secret—don't tell Mom and Dad!)

My grandma likes me to help her around the house. She calls me her "little helper."

I don't know how she manages when I'm not here.

Grandma never gets angry, even when I make a terrible mess. And she always likes my cooking.

I can't wait for her to taste my cupcakes.

Grandma doesn't mind how much noise I make. She even bought me a wonderful set of drums. Won't Mom and Dad be pleased?

My grandma has plenty of interesting hobbies. She's the coolest grandma I know.

And she knits me fabulous sweaters.

(Well... my toy giraffe likes the sweaters, anyway.)

My grandma loves playing games. She likes tons of games, but her favorite game of all is hide-and-seek.

I normally hide and she looks for me.

I'm so good at hiding that she never finds me. Or at least she pretends she can't find me, even when I think she knows where I am.

At bedtime, Grandma tells me funny stories about Dad when he was a little boy. She says that he was a real prankster.

I don't believe that Dad was ever bad, but the stories make me laugh anyway. She makes me laugh so much that I get hiccups.

But my grandma's so great that she knows exactly how to get rid of them.

I'm always sad when I kiss Grandma good-bye. But she only lives next door, so I visit her whenever I want because... my grandma is *great!*

Lucy Locket

Lucy Locket lost her pocket,
Kitty Fisher found it.
Not a penny was there in it,
Only ribbon round it.

Ice Cream

Ice cream, ice cream, a penny a lump!
The more you eat, the more you jump.

If Pigs Could Fly

If pigs could fly
High in the sky,
Where do you think they'd go?
Would they follow an airplane
To France or Spain,
Or drift where the wind blows?

The Wind

When the wind is in the East,
'Tis neither good to man nor beast.
When the wind is in the North,
The skillful fisher goes not forth.
When the wind is in the South,
It blows the bait in the fish's mouth.
When the wind is in the West,
Then it is at its very best.

Kindness

If I had a donkey that would not go,
Would I beat him? Oh no, no.
I'd put him in the barn and give him some corn,
The best little donkey that ever was born.

Little Friend

In the greenhouse lives a wren,
Little friend of little men;
When they're good she tells them where
To find the apple, quince, and pear.

Cinderella

Once upon a time, there was a pretty young girl who lived with her father, stepmother, and two stepsisters. The stepmother was unkind, and the stepsisters were mean.

Every day, the girl got up at dawn to cook and clean and wash and sew for her stepmother and stepsisters. Every night, the stepmother told the girl to sleep beside the fire. Soon the girl's clothes and hair were so gray with ash and cinders that everyone called her **Cinderella**.

One morning, a special invitation arrived. All the young women in the kingdom were invited to a ball at the royal palace so that the young prince could choose a bride.

The two stepsisters were very excited and ordered Cinderella around as she helped them get ready for the ball. Cinderella **sighed**. She wished she

could go with them. As an elegant carriage took her stepsisters to the ball, Cinderella sat beside the hearth and wept.

"I wish I could go to the ball," she cried.

Suddenly, a strange light filled the room. Cinderella looked up. A silvery glow surrounded a kind-looking woman with a glittering wand.

"Who are you?" asked Cinderella, blinking in wonder.

"I am your **fairy godmother**," she said. "I've come to help you go to the ball."

"But how?" asked Cinderella.

"Find me a big pumpkin, a white mouse, and a rat," replied the fairy godmother.

Cinderella found everything as quickly as she could. The fairy godmother waved her wand. The pumpkin changed into a **magnificent** golden coach, the white mouse became a white horse, and the rat became a coachman.

With one last gentle tap of the wand, Cinderella's dusty dress became a shimmering ball gown. On her feet were two **sparkling** glass slippers.

"Now," said the fairy godmother, "you are ready for the ball. But at the stroke of midnight, the magic will end, and everything will return to what it was."

Cinderella promised to be home before midnight.

When Cinderella arrived at the palace, everyone turned to look at her. No one knew who Cinderella was, not even her own stepsisters.

The prince thought that she was the loveliest, most enchanting girl he had ever seen. He danced only with her.

As Cinderella whirled around the room in his arms, she felt so happy that she forgot her fairy godmother's warning.

Suddenly, she heard the clock chime … once, twice

… **twelve times!**

"I must go!" cried Cinderella. And before the prince could stop her, she ran from the ballroom and out of the palace.

"Wait!" cried the prince, dashing after her. But by the time he reached the palace steps, she was gone.

Then he saw something twinkling on the steps, a single glass slipper. The prince picked it up.

"I will marry the woman whose foot fits this glass slipper," he declared. "I will search the kingdom until I find her."

The next day, the prince began going from house to house, looking for his true love. Every young woman in the kingdom tried on the glass slipper, but it didn't fit anyone.

At last, the prince came to Cinderella's house.

Her stepsisters were waiting to try on the slipper.

The first stepsister pushed and squeezed, but she could barely get her fat toes into the tiny slipper.

The second stepsister also tried to cram her foot into the shoe. But it was no use.

The prince was turning to leave when a soft voice asked, "May I try the slipper, please?"

As Cinderella stepped forward to try on the slipper, her stepsisters began to laugh.

"Everyone should have a chance," said the prince, as he held out the sparkling slipper. And suddenly...

"Oh!" gasped her stepsisters.

Cinderella's dainty foot fitted into the slipper perfectly. As her stepsisters gazed in amazement, the prince joyfully took Cinderella in his arms.

Her stepsisters and stepmother were still trembling with shock as they watched Cinderella ride off in the prince's own carriage.

Cinderella and the prince were soon married, and lived happily ever after.

Bunny Helps Mommy

It was a good day to dry some laundry. The sun was shining and the wind was blowing.

Bunny was helping his mommy by hanging out the laundry on the line.

Suddenly the wind blew extra-hard, and it whisked some of the laundry away.

"Come back!" cried Bunny, and he chased the laundry as it flipped and flapped off through the woods.

He found two noisy birds squabbling over his stripy socks. They wanted to take the socks to line their nests with and make them all cozy for the baby birds.

"I want those back, thank you!" cried Bunny.

Then Bunny saw something moving along the ground.

It was brightly colored.

It looked like Daddy's woolly hat, but it was moving!

Bunny cautiously lifted the hat up. Some furry mice peeped out from underneath. They were taking it away to make a soft bed with.

"I want that back, thank you!" cried Bunny.

Then Bunny noticed the corner of his baby brother's special blanket poking out from a hole in a tree.

He pulled as hard as he could until out popped the blanket, and out popped a family of furry squirrels. They had been using the blanket to snuggle up in.

"I want that back, thank you!" cried Bunny.

Bunny gathered up all the laundry in the wood, until he had a big wobbly pile.

He took it all home and he hung it back on the line. It was hard work for a little bunny like him.

When Mommy came outside, all the laundry was dry. And Bunny was curled up in the laundry basket... fast asleep!

Pajama Party Disco

It was the school vacation. Hannah, Emma, and Ashley were at Deisha's for a sleepover.

"Let's have a disco!" said Deisha as they munched on some potato chips. "We can use my new disco ball lamp."

"Great idea!" said the others.

Deisha got out her best music for dancing to, and the others looked through Deisha's closet for party clothes to wear.

Once they had all changed, the girls cleared a space on Deisha's bedroom floor and closed the curtains. Deisha put on the music and Ashley switched on the disco ball lamp.

The girls started to sing and dance. Deisha picked up her hairbrush and jumped onto her bed. "Look at me!" she laughed. "I could be a popstar!" Her friends cheered as she sang along, pretending the hairbrush was a microphone.

Before long, Ashley, Hannah, and Emma were singing and dancing on the bed, too.

Just as Hannah was in the middle of a high kick there was a loud cracking noise and Deisha's bed collapsed.

Emma and Ashley landed on the floor in a heap, and Hannah tripped forwards and crashed into Deisha.

Deisha's big brother Jon came rushing into the room. "What's going on in here?" he grinned. "Disco dancing accident?"

"It's not funny!" said Deisha. "We've broken the bed!"

"I could mend it," said Jon. "I might not even tell Mom. What's it worth?"

The girls looked at each other. "How about half a bar of chocolate?" said Emma.

Jon laughed. "No way! You'll have to do better than that!"

In the end the girls had to promise Jon *all* their candy and potato chips before he went to get the toolbox.

When Jon had fixed the bed, the girls got into their pajamas.

"The next time I'm disco dancing, it's going to be on a proper dance floor!" groaned Deisha. "Or a stage in front of a huge audience!" laughed Ashley.

The Fairies

Up the airy mountain,
Down the rushy glen,
We daren't go a-hunting
For fear of little men;
Wee folk, good folk,
Trooping all together;
Green jacket, red cap,
And a white owl's feather!

Down along the rocky shore
Some make their home,
They live on crispy pancakes
Of yellow tide foam;
Some in the reeds
Of the black mountain lake,
With frogs for their watchdogs,
All night awake.

By the craggy hill-side,
Through the mosses bare,
They have planted thorn-trees
For pleasure here and there.
If any man so daring
As dig them up in spite,
He shall find their sharpest thorns
In his bed at night.

The Butterfly's Ball

Come take up your hats, and away let us haste
To the butterfly's ball, and the grasshopper's feast.
The trumpeter gadfly has summoned the crew,
And the revels are now only waiting for you.

On the smooth shaven grass by the side of a wood,
Beneath a broad oak that for ages has stood,
See the children of earth, and the tenants of air,
For an evening's amusement together repair.

And there came the moth, with his plumage of down,
And the hornet in jacket of yellow and brown;
Who with him the wasp, his companion, did bring,
But they promised, that evening, to lay by their sting.

With step so majestic the snail did advance,
And promised the gazers a minuet to dance.
But they all laughed so loud that he pulled in his head,
And went in his own little chamber to bed.

Then, as evening gave way to the shadows of night,
Their watchman, the glow-worm, came out with a light.
Then home let us hasten, while yet we can see,
For no watchman is waiting for you and for me.

Just as Well, Really!

Rumpus liked water. He liked the drippiness and droppiness, the splashiness and sloppiness of it!

He liked it so much that, whenever there was water around, Rumpus somehow always managed to fall into it!

But Mom loved Rumpus, so she simply sighed and she mopped up the mess.

Rumpus loved mud. He loved the way you could plodge in it, splodge in it, slide in it, and glide in it!

Rumpus somehow always managed to get covered in it!

But Dad loved Rumpus, so every time he simply sighed and he sponged off the splatters.

Rumpus enjoyed paint. He liked to splatter and dash it, to spread and splash it! Rumpus somehow managed to get it everywhere!

But Rumpus's big brother loved him, so every time he simply sighed and cleaned him up.

Rumpus loved his mom, dad, and big brother.

Rumpus's mom, dad, brother and loved Rumpus... which was just as well, really!

Clara Cow's Cold

One morning, Clara Cow woke up with a tickle in her nose.

"*Aaaa-tishoo!* Oh dear," said Clara. "I think I've caught a nasty cold."

"You should borrow the scarecrow's hat," squeaked the mice. And off they scurried to fetch it.

"*Aaaa-tishoo!* Thank you!" sneezed Clara, even louder, as she put it on."

"You must keep warm," clucked Harriet the hen. "Why don't you borrow that scarf on the laundry line?"

"*Aaaa-tishoo!* Good idea!" sneezed Clara, wrapping it round her neck.

Then she sneezed loudly again.

Her loud sneeze woke Danny the duck. "If you've got a cold, you need rain boots to keep your feet dry!" he quacked.

"*Aaaa-tishoo!* That might do the trick!" agreed Clara. "I'll borrow the farmer's boots." And she slipped them on.

But Clara just kept on sneezing. "*Aaaa-tishoo!*"

"Time for bed!" ordered her friends, and Clara agreed.

"*Aaaaa….*" began Clara, as she snuggled down. But no sneeze came, just a *big* yawn.

And when Clara woke the next morning her cold was gone!

Utterly Crazy

Did you ever see a piglet all dressed up in polka dots,
Or a princess on her wedding day break out in bright green spots?
Did you ever see a colonel drinking coffee with a horse,
Or a three-legged mongoose? It's very rare, of course.
And if you've never visited a pink giraffe who's lazy,
Then you, my friend, are totally, utterly crazy!

The Cherry Tree

Once I found a cherry pit,
I put it in the ground,
And when I came to look at it,
A tiny shoot I found.

The shoot grew up and up each day,
And soon became a tree.
I picked the rosy cherries then,
And ate them one, two, three.

The Apple Tree

Here is the tree with leaves so green.
Here are the apples that hang between.
When the wind blows the apples fall.
Here is a basket to gather them all.

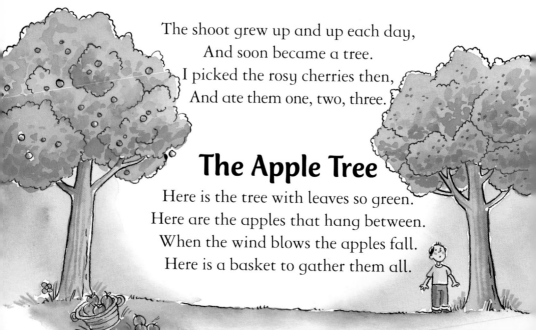

I Had a Little Nut Tree

I had a little nut tree, nothing would it bear,
But a silver nutmeg and a golden pear;
The King of Spain's daughter came to visit me,
And all for the sake of my little nut tree.

Little Fishes

Little fishes in a brook,
Father caught them on a hook,
Mother fried them in a pan,
Johnnie eats them like a man.

Ickle Ockle

Ickle ockle, blue bockle,
Fishes in the sea,
If you want a pretty maid,
Please choose me.

I'm a Big Sister!

Emily was Mommy's and Daddy's little girl. But one day Mommy went into the hospital – and when she came back she had a new baby with her.

"Now you're a big sister!" Mommy told Emily.

Everyone made a big fuss of the new baby.

"Baby's so little!" Auntie Molly said. "Isn't it lovely to be a big sister?"

"Yes," said Emily. But she wasn't so sure. Sometimes she wished she could be little again, like Baby.

When Baby's diaper needed changing, Emily asked Mommy, "Did I wear a diaper too?"

Mommy smiled. "Yes you did, Emily. But now you're too grown-up for diapers. Big sisters wear underpants. Yours have flowers on them."

"And I can put them on myself," said Emily.

"That's right," said Mommy. "But Baby still needs a lot of help—not like you!"

"Can I help change Baby's diaper?" Emily asked.

"Of course," said Mommy. "Thank you. Baby's very lucky to have a big sister who helps!"

But Emily still thought it might be fun to be as little as Baby.

The next day, when Daddy got the baby's bottle ready, Emily asked, "Did I have my dinner in a bottle, too?"

Daddy smiled. "Yes, Emily," he said. "But now you're too grown-up for a bottle. Big sisters eat sandwiches and drink milk from a cup."

"And I can eat sandwiches and drink milk all by myself!" said Emily. "I don't need anyone to help me."

"Of course you can," said Daddy. "That's what big sisters do. But Baby still needs a lot of help."

"Can I help feed the baby?" Emily asked Daddy.

"I think Baby would like that very much," said Daddy. "Baby's so lucky to have such a helpful big sister!"

That night, Emily watched Mommy put Baby to sleep.

"Did I sleep in a crib like Baby's?" she asked.

"Yes, Emily, you did. But now you're too grown-up for a crib," said Mommy. "Big sisters sleep in big, cozy beds, just like yours."

Emily looked at her bed. With its pretty quilt and a huge pile of cuddly toys, it really did look cozy.

"There are no animals in Baby's crib," Emily said. "Let's give Baby my yellow bunny—just for now."

"That's very kind of you, Emily," said Mommy. "Baby is lucky to have a big sister who shares!"

The next day, Emily and Mommy went out to the park. Baby came too, in a stroller.

"Did I ride in a stroller like Baby?" Emily asked.

"Yes, you did," replied Mommy. "But you're a big sister now. Big sisters can walk—and run and jump. Baby can't do any of those things yet. Baby's lucky to have a strong, big sister like you!"

At the park, Emily saw the ice-cream truck.

I'm a Big Sister!

"Will you buy an ice cream for Baby?" she asked Mommy.

"No, Emily," said Mommy. "Baby's too little for ice cream. But her big sister isn't! What flavor would you like?"

"Chocolate!" said Emily. "Thank you!"

Emily looked at Baby, and Baby smiled at her.

Emily smiled, too.

"I'm glad we have a baby," she told Mommy. "I get to help, and share and push the stroller—and I get to have ice cream, too! Being a big sister is… the best!"

A Friend for Barney

It was Saturday morning at Prairie Farm. Robin, Jennifer, and Marley the dog went down to the pond to feed the ducks.

"All the ducks are friends," said Jennifer. "They never fight about who gets the biggest piece of bread."

"Not like you," said Robin.

"That's because you always get the biggest piece," said Jennifer.

When they went to see the chickens, Robin asked, "Are they friends, too?"

"I think so," said Jennifer, "but some of them peck a bit."

"What about the pigs? Sometimes Bessie can be a bit grumpy with her piglets," said Robin.

"Oh, that's just because she is their mom," said Jennifer, "and they are very greedy sometimes so Bessie has to tell them off."

"Everybody at Prairie Farm has friends," agreed Robin.

"Stan is mine," said Jennifer.

"Cats are boring," declared Robin. "They just sleep all the time. My best friend is Marley. He's the fastest dog in the world!"

"But Barney the scarecrow doesn't have a friend," said Jennifer, frowning. "He just stands on the hill all day with no one to talk to."

When they went back to the house, Jennifer said to her mom, "Barney's lonely."

"Then why don't you make him a friend?" asked Mom. That afternoon, she took them to a garage sale so they could get some clothes for a new scarecrow. Robin found an old pair of sports shoes and a pair of leather gloves. Jennifer found a pink party dress and a hat with a green ribbon.

Robin stuffed an old sack with straw and Dad helped Jennifer to paint a face at the top. Mom made some hair out of yarn.

"What a beauty," said Dad. "All she needs is a name."

"I want to call her Mary, like my doll," said Jennifer.

"Scary Mary Crow," said Robin. "That's a great name."

So, that's what they called her. They took Scary Mary up the hill.

"Hello, Barney," said Robin. "We've brought you a friend."

"Now you won't be lonely anymore," added Jennifer.

"I think Barney likes her," said Robin. "He can see by looking at the shoes she's wearing that she's very good at soccer."

"I think he likes her because she has a smiley face," said Jennifer.

Jennifer skipped all the way home to tell Stan the cat all about Scary Mary.

"I'm very happy, Stan," she said, giving him a big hug. "Now everybody at Prairie Farm has a friend."

Nibbling Neighbors

One sunny morning in the meadow, Alice was happily munching away when she was surprised to discover a hole where there should be grass.

"My dears," she mooed, "there's a hole in our field!"

The next morning, where there had been one hole before, now there were five!

"If this goes on," said Bryony, "we'll have nowhere to stand!"

"And nothing to eat," added Rowan, sounding alarmed.

By the end of the week, there were over a hundred holes.

"You've got some nibbling neighbors," said Farmer Jim. "It looks like a family of rabbits has come to stay."

The cows shuddered. "Those hopping things with long ears?" asked Holly. "I can't look my best with them around!"

"And they have very, very large families," warned Rowan. "Not just one baby at a time, like cows do."

"It's odd we've never seen one," said Bryony thoughtfully. "I'm going to keep watch tonight."

That night, as the full moon rose over the meadow, Bryony pretended to go to sleep. Although she was expecting it, she was shocked when two bright eyes and a twitchy nose popped up in front of her.

"*Aaaaaghh!*" cried Bryony.
"*Aaaaaghh!*" cried the
rabbit, and disappeared
down its hole.

"You should have followed
it!" cried Alice, who had been
woken by the sudden noise.

"Down a rabbit hole?" gasped Rowan.
"Don't be silly, Alice. She's far too big!"

"Then we're doomed," said Holly, gloomily. "Those rabbits
will take over without us even seeing them do it."

The next morning, the cows awoke to an amazing sight.
Hundreds of rabbits were sitting around them.

"Excuse me!" said the largest
one. "We've come to ask for
your help."

"Help?" echoed Alice.
"We're the ones who need
help!"

The rabbit explained that
his family lived in fear. "Your hoofs
are so big, you could stamp on us without noticing."

Just then, Bryony had one of her excellent ideas. "You would
be much safer," she said, "if you lived under the hedges."

So they did. All day in the meadow, there's munching, and
mooing. All night in the hedges, there's nibbling, digging, and
wiggling. And everyone is happy.

My Mother Said

My mother said I never should
Play with the gypsies in the wood.

If I did, then she would say,
"Naughty girl to disobey!

Your hair won't curl and your shoes won't shine,
You gypsy girl, you won't be mine!"

The wood was dark; the grass was green.
In came Sally with a tambourine.

I crept to the sea—no ship to get across,
I paid ten quarters for a blind white horse.

I got up on his back and was off in a crack!
Sally, tell my mother I will never come back.

Bed in Summer

In winter I get up at night
And dress by yellow candlelight.
In summer quite the other way,
I have to go to bed by day.

I have to go to bed and see
The birds still hopping on the tree,
Or hear the grown-up people's feet
Still going past me in the street.

And does it not seem hard to you,
When all the sky is clear and blue,
And I should like so much to play,
To have to go to bed by day?

Snoozy Princess Susie

Z - Z - Z - Z - z

Princess Susie was so perfect in almost every way.
She always fed her dragon, Spark, and put her clothes away.
She never ever said rude words, or disobeyed the queen.
Her bedroom was the tidiest that you have ever seen!

But Susie did do something that made her mother weep.
No matter what the time of day, poor Susie fell asleep!
She fell asleep at breakfast time, and in the banquet hall.
She often dozed upon the stairs, all curled up in a ball.

The queen was beside herself. "The answer's plain," she said.
"If Susie just can't keep awake, she must go straight to bed!"
But though she went to bed at six, and didn't rise 'til nine,
Susie yawned and snored all day, no matter what the time.

No one knew quite what to do to put the matter right,
'Til clever fairy Heather saw something strange one night.
As she flew home in the dark she heard a gentle sigh.
There was Susie, wide awake, gazing at the sky!

"I love to watch the stars," she said, "and see the shining moon!
I'd rather be here, counting stars, than sleeping in my room!"
Heather smiled and waved her wand. "I have a plan!" she said.
As if by magic shining stars appeared above the bed.

Now Susie watches stars in bed to help her get to sleep.
She counts them as they float above, instead of counting sheep!

Birthday Sleepover

It was Hannah's birthday and she had invited her friends to a special sleepover. Because it was a warm summer evening, they were going to camp in the backyard in Hannah's new tent. They had been looking forward to it for weeks and were planning a special midnight feast.

The moon was shining brightly as the girls settled into the tent. Hannah, Emma, and Deisha zipped up the door and climbed into their sleeping bags.

"It's such a pity Ashley couldn't come," said Emma. "This is going to be so much fun!"

They unpacked their feast of potato chips, cookies and peanut-butter sandwiches. As they tucked in, they made each other laugh with spooky ghost stories.

Deisha began telling them about an old barn nearby. Her brother had said it was haunted.

Then there was a bang from outside the tent.

"What was that?" asked Emma, looking worried.

"Just a cat, or something," said Hannah, nervously.

They all listened again. There was another bang and then a noise that sounded like a twig snapping. Emma jumped. "That wasn't a cat!" she said, grabbing her flashlight.

"What's that strange rustling noise?" said Deisha.

Hannah reached for her shoes. "I don't like this!" she said.

"Let's get out of here!" yelled Deisha.

The girls grabbed their things and squeezed out of the tent.

"Quick! Follow me!" shouted Hannah. She began to lead them across the grass toward the house.

"Wait!" said a voice behind them. "Where are you all going?" It was Ashley!

"My mom said I could come after all!" Ashley laughed. "But it was hard to find your tent in the dark."

Hannah, Deisha, and Emma laughed. "So it was you making all those noises!" said Deisha. "Not a ghost at all!"

Hannah hugged Ashley. "I'm so glad you're here," she said. "It wouldn't have been a proper birthday without you."

"Now let's finish off this midnight feast!" cried Emma.

The Enchanted Garden

Princess Sylvie loved to walk through the meadows to look at the flowers.

One day she found an overgrown path in her favorite meadow. She asked a woman where the path led.

"To the garden of the enchantress!" said the woman. "You can go and look, but they say that whatever you do, don't pick the flowers."

Princess Sylvie followed the path until she came to a small house with the prettiest garden she had ever seen, filled with flowers of every color and scent.

Princess Sylvie went back to the garden every day. Soon she forgot all about the enchantress—and one day, she picked a rose from the garden and took it back to the castle. As she put it in water, Princess Sylvie suddenly remembered the warning!

But months passed and nothing happened. The rose stayed as fresh as the day it was picked. Forgetting her fears, Princess Sylvie went back to the enchanted garden.

When she saw the garden, Princess Sylvie wanted to cry. The grass was brown. All the flowers had withered.

Then she heard someone weeping. Inside the house the enchantress was sitting by the fire, crying. She was old and bent. Princess Sylvie was afraid, but she felt sorry for her.

"What happened to your lovely garden?" Princess Sylvie asked.

"Someone picked a rose from it!" said the enchantress. "The garden is under a spell: the picked flower will live forever, but the rest of the flowers must die! And when the rose was picked, my magic was lost, too, and I too am beginning to wither and die!"

"What can I do?" said Princess Sylvie, heartbroken.

"Only a princess can help," she replied. "She must bring me six sacks of stinging nettles! And no princess would do that!"

Princess Sylvie gathered six sacks of nettles, not caring that they stung her, and took them back to the enchantress.

The enchantress said, "But the nettles must be picked by a princess."

"I am a princess," said Princess Sylvie.

The enchantress made a magic potion with the nettles and drank it. Instantly, the garden became beautiful again—and Princess Sylvie gasped! Gone was the bent old lady. In her place was a beautiful young woman.

"My garden is restored," smiled the enchantress, "and so am I!"

And so the enchantress and the princess became good friends and shared the enchanted garden.

Can I See Another's Woe?

Can I see another's woe,
And not be in sorrow, too?
Can I see another's grief,
And not seek for kind relief?

Bob Robin

Little Bob Robin,
Where do you live?
Up in yonder wood, sir,
On a hazel twig.

Old Farmer Giles

Old Farmer Giles,
He went seven miles
With his faithful dog Old Rover;
And his faithful dog Old Rover,
When he came to the stiles,
Took a run, and jumped clean over.

Red Stockings

Red stockings, blue stockings,
Shoes tied up with silver;
A red rosette upon my breast
And a gold ring on my finger.

Fidget

As little Jenny Wren
Was sitting by the shed,
She waggled with her tail,
She nodded with her head;
She waggled with her tail,
She nodded with her head;
As Little Jenny Wren
Was sitting by the shed.

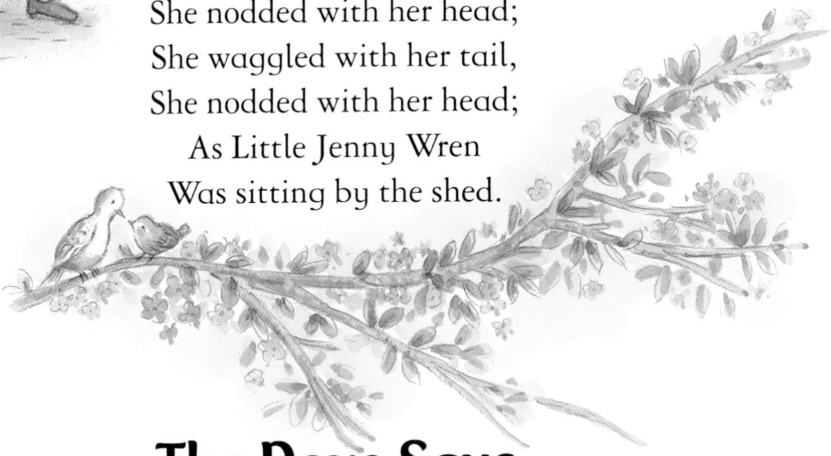

The Dove Says

The dove says, "Coo, coo! What should I do?
I can scarce maintain two."
"Pooh, pooh," says the wren, "I have ten,
And keep them all like gentlemen.
Curr dhoo, curr dhoo! Love me and I'll love you!"

Dreams

Beyond, beyond the mountain line,
The gray stone and the boulder,
Beyond the growth of dark green pine,
That crowns its western shoulder,
There lies that fairy land of mine,
Unseen of a beholder.

Its fruits are all like rubies rare,
Its streams are clear as glasses:
There golden castles hang in air,
And purple grapes in masses,
And noble knights and ladies fair
Come riding down the passes.

Ah me! They say if I could stand
Upon those mountain ledges,
I should but see on either hand
Plain fields and dusty hedges:
And yet I know my fairy land
Lies somewhere o'er their hedges.

Three Little Kittens

Three little kittens,
They lost their mittens,
And they began to cry,
"Oh, mother dear,
We sadly fear
Our mittens we have lost."

"What? Lost your mittens,
You naughty kittens!
Then you shall have no pie.
Meow, meow, meow, meow.
No, you shall have no pie."

The three little kittens,
They found their mittens,
And they began to smile,
"Oh, mother dear,
See here, see here,
Our mittens we have found."

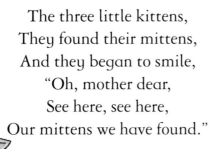

"What? Found your mittens,
You clever kittens!
Then you shall have some pie.
Purr, purr, purr, purr.
Oh, let us have some pie."

My Dad Is Great

My dad is great.

 We have tons of fun together. Today, Mom and Baby are going shopping with Grandma for the day, so Dad and I have all day to spend together. I'm so excited!

I can't wait to see what adventures Dad has planned for me while they're away.

My dad is very patient. He always lets me choose all of my own clothes.

He doesn't care how long it takes. I think that, secretly, he really enjoys it! (I wonder if he would like me to help choose his clothes?)

My dad often picks me up from school. He's bigger and stronger than all the other dads.

And he's a fantastic sailor. He's got a beautiful white yacht.

My Dad Is Great.

It's the fastest boat on the pond in the park down the road.

He's a great sport. He always lets me win when we play baseball. (But I pretend not to notice.)

Dad and I like the same things. Hot dogs are our very favorite food in the whole wide world.

My dad's ever so funny. He always makes me laugh.

My dad's a fast runner. He runs around the park much quicker than everyone else.

When Dad's around, everything seems fun.

Even cleaning and tidying up!

When they get home, I tell Mom and Baby about the amazing things we've been doing. I can't wait until Baby is old enough to hear all about Dad.

Because although all dads are special, my dad is... *great*!

An Angel of My Own

Alyssa was a pretty little girl who lived with her mom, her dad and her baby brother Matthew.

Alyssa looked as good and sweet as a little angel, but she didn't always act like one. Sometimes, she could be very bad indeed.

One afternoon, Alyssa's grandma came for lunch. Grandma was very pleased to see Alyssa and baby Matthew.

"Alyssa, please kiss your grandma," said Mom. But Alyssa ran away from Grandma into the backyard.

Later that evening, Alyssa wanted to play.

"Please play quietly, Alyssa," Mom said. "Matthew is asleep."

But Alyssa started jumping loudly across the floor.

Stamp! Stamp! Stamp! went Alyssa's feet. Matthew woke up and began to cry.

"Stop crying, Matthew," ordered Alyssa. She made a face at him. Matthew cried even harder.

"Please be nice to Matthew," Mom said, when she saw what Alyssa was doing. Alyssa stuck out her tongue rudely.

That night, Alyssa felt unhappy. She thought about all the bad things she'd done. She wished she could make everything all right.

In the middle of the night, Alyssa was sleeping peacefully. Suddenly, a strange glow filled the room. Alyssa opened her eyes and next to her bed was a beautiful angel. The angel had a kind face and wonderful, shimmering wings.

"Hi, Alyssa," smiled the angel. "Don't be afraid. I know that you're feeling a bit sad. I've come to try and help you."

The angel took Alyssa by the hand. "Let's talk about all the things that have happened today, and think about how we could have made them better. It would make your grandma so happy if you would spend time with her."

"I didn't mean to run away from Grandma," said Alyssa.

"And what about baby Matthew?" asked the angel. "If you accidentally wake him up, why don't you try and make him laugh instead of cry?"

Alyssa nodded her head happily. That was a good idea. Alyssa felt much better.

The angel tucked Alyssa back into bed and stroked her face tenderly.

"I wish I could be a beautiful angel like you one day," Alyssa whispered.

The angel smiled. "Well Alyssa, you have to be very good to become an angel," she replied. "But I'm sure you can do it if you try."

Alyssa nodded her head. "Yes, I think I can," she said. "I'll be much nicer from now on."

The next afternoon, Alyssa's grandma came to lunch. Without being asked, Alyssa ran up to her and gave her a big kiss.

"Hi, Alyssa!" said Grandma happily. "It's lovely to see you."

Alyssa and Grandma had a wonderful time. Alyssa drew Grandma a special picture, which she was very pleased with. Then they played nice games together.

At lunchtime, everyone enjoyed all the lovely food Alyssa's mom had made.

That evening, after Grandma had gone home, Alyssa wanted to play.

"Please play quietly," said Mom. "Matthew's sleeping."

Alyssa had wanted to play noisily. She started to jump across the floor, but then she remembered what the angel had said.

Matthew hadn't woken up, so Alyssa tiptoed silently across the room and chose a book from the shelf. She sat quietly on a bean bag to look at it.

Alyssa didn't make a single sound.

As the days and weeks passed by, Alyssa was hardly bad at all.

One day, Mom and Dad had a special surprise for her.

"We're very proud of you," said Dad, giving Alyssa a big hug. "You've been such a good girl lately, we've got you a present."

Dad handed Alyssa a box. Inside was a beautiful silver necklace. There was an angel charm hanging from it.

"A little angel for our little angel," said Mom. She put the necklace around Alyssa's neck.

"Oh! Thank you, Mom!" beamed Alyssa as she gave her mom a great big hug.

The Seasons

In the winter comes the snow,
Makes our feet and fingers glow.
Early spring brings the rain,
Thaws the frozen ponds again.
Then come breezes, loud and shrill,
They stir the dancing daffodil.
Soon flowers the primrose sweet,
Daisies scatter at our feet.
See the flocks of pretty lambs,
Skipping by their fleecy dams!
Summer brings tulips, lilies, roses;
Fills the children's hands and posies.
Then it brings us cooling showers,
Strawberries and gilly flowers.
The sun ripens sheaves of corn,
Then the harvest home is borne.
In the cool fall comes the pheasant;
Then to gather nuts is pleasant.
But all too soon come icy blasts,
Then the leaves are falling fast.
In the winter comes the snow,
Makes our feet and fingers glow.

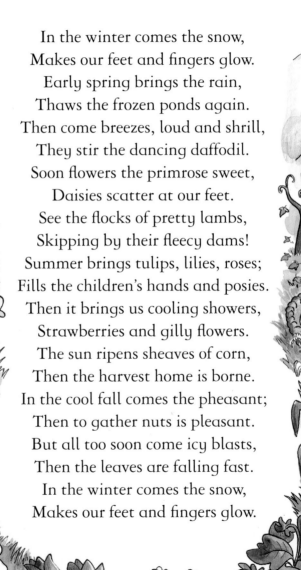

The Moon

The moon has a face like the clock in the hall;
She shines on thieves on the garden wall,
On streets and fields and harbor quays,
And birdies asleep in the forks of the trees.

The squalling cat and the squeaking mouse,
The howling dog by the door of the house,
The bat that lies in bed at noon,
All love to be out by the light of the moon.

But all of the things that belong to the day
Cuddle to sleep to be out of her way;
And flowers and children close their eyes
'Til up in the morning the sun shall arise.

In Lincoln Lane

I lost my mare in Lincoln Lane,
I'll never find her there again;
She lost a shoe, and then lost two,
And threw her rider in the drain.

Charley Barley

Charley Barley, butter and eggs,
Sold his wife for three duck eggs.
When the ducks began to lay,
Charley Barley flew away.

Five Little Ducks

Five little ducks went swimming one day,
Over the hills and far away,
Mother Duck said, "Quack, quack, quack, quack,"
But only four little ducks came back.
Four little ducks went swimming one day,
Over the hills and far away,
Mother Duck said, "Quack, quack, quack, quack,"
But only three little ducks came back.

(continue with three little ducks, etc.)

There Was an Old Crow

There was an old crow
Sat upon a clod.
There's an end of my song,
That's odd!

Birds of a Feather

Birds of a feather flock together,
And so will pigs and swine;
Rats and mice shall have their choice,
And so will I have mine.

The Wise Old Owl

There was an old owl who lived in an oak;
The more he heard, the less he spoke.
The less he spoke, the more he heard.
Why aren't we like that wise old bird?

Sleepover Splash

In Ashley's bedroom Hannah, Emma, and Deisha were rolling out their sleeping bags for another sleepover.

"Max is driving me mad!" said Ashley. "I hate having a twin brother!"

All day long Max had been playing jokes on Ashley. He and his friend James had put a frog in her bed and spread mustard in her peanut-butter sandwiches. They had also hidden her ballet shoes so she was late for her lesson.

"Why don't you get back?" said Deisha. She sat down on Ashley's bed. "Let's come up with a joke to play on him!"

Emma and Hannah agreed.

"I know!" said Deisha. "Here's a good joke! Let's put a

bucket of water above his door. When he opens it he'll get soaked!"

"That's a great idea!" said Ashley, jumping up. "I'll go and get a bucket from downstairs and you all make sure Max is out of his room!"

Emma and Hannah went out onto

the landing and knocked on Max's door. There was no answer. "All clear!" they called. Ashley came back up with the bucket, and she and Deisha took it to the bathroom to fill it with water.

Deisha climbed onto a chair and lifted up the bucket.

Ashley opened Max's door just enough so the bucket would balance on top. "Max!" she called. "There's something in your room for you!"

Ashley, Hannah, and Emma raced across the landing, back to Ashley's bedroom. "Quick, Deisha!" hissed Ashley.

But just as Max came up the stairs, Deisha lost her balance on the chair and, with a loud cry, tumbled down onto Max. The bucket toppled over, soaking them both from head to toe in icy cold water!

Mina's Lucky Shoes

Mina loved ballet. She went to the Starlight Ballet School. She had a ballet class every week.

Mina loved her ballet teacher, Miss Silver.

"You dance very well, Mina," said Miss Silver.

Mina was very happy—except for one thing. She found one of the dance steps very hard!

When Mina had to spin around very fast it made her dizzy. Sometimes she even fell over!

"Try again, Mina," said Miss Silver. "Keep your head in one place as you are spinning, and then turn it around quickly at the last minute. You will do it."

Mina tried again, but she just couldn't get the hang of it. Spinning still made her dizzy.

"I'll never be able to spin," she said sadly to her mom.

"I have an idea," said Mom. She went up to the attic. When she came back down again she was holding an old box.

She gave the box to Mina. There were some yellow ballet shoes inside. They were made of the most beautiful satin, but they were very old.

"Wow!" said Mina. "Whose are these?"

"These were my lucky ballet shoes when I was your age," said her mom.

Mina put on the yellow ballet shoes. They fitted perfectly.

Then she tried a spin. She thought hard about what Miss Silver had told her. She turned her head at the last minute. And Mina didn't feel dizzy!

"They are lucky!" she said to Mom.

Mom laughed. "Maybe they are," she said. "Or maybe you've just learned how to spin.

"They are definitely lucky," said Mina.

Mina wore the yellow ballet shoes for her next class. Her spinning was perfect.

"Well done, Mina," said Miss Silver.

Mina was delighted!

Good Girl, Molly

Molly's mom Meg was a sheepdog. She helped Farmer Peter round up the sheep.

"Good girl, Meg," Peter would say almost every day.

Molly was too small to help. Whenever she tried to help, Farmer Peter would say, "Stay here, Molly."

Molly was bored of watching Mom round up sheep. She wanted to help, too. She wanted Farmer Peter to say, "Good girl, Molly," to her, too.

One day, Meg was helping Farmer Peter to put all the sheep into a big pen.

"Good girl, Meg," said Farmer Peter, closing the gate and patting Meg on the head. But as he turned away a lamb slipped through the last crack in the gate and ran away.

Meg did not see. But Molly saw the lamb. She ran after it.

"Where is Molly?" said Farmer Peter, a few minutes later.

Then he heard barking coming from the top field.

The silly lamb had got itself stuck in a hedge. Farmer Peter saw Molly barking next to the lamb.

"Good girl, Molly," he said.

Goldy and the Jacket

"Bad Goldy!" Grace the farmer would cry almost every day, as she came out to get the laundry to find the goat munching on a towel or chomping on a sock.

But Goldy wouldn't stop. She just loved eating laundry!

One day there was a green jacket hanging on the line.

"Tasty!" thought Goldy. Soon she had munched it all up.

It wasn't long before Goldy started to feel ill.

"Has she eaten anything unusual?" the vet asked Grace.

Grace gasped. "My waterproof jacket! When I brought the clothes in it was gone. She must have eaten it. Poor Goldy!"

The vet laughed. "Goats have tough stomachs," he said. "She'll feel better soon." He patted Goldy on the head. "And that'll teach you to eat things goats aren't supposed to eat!"

"Baaa!" agreed Goldy.

Just as the vet said, Goldy was soon feeling better.

"Grass is enough for me from now on!" she said to herself, chewing a mouthful. "No more laundry for Goldy."

Then she looked over at the laundry line. There was a tasty-looking red sock hanging on it.

"Well, maybe just one last sock..." she thought.

Fishes Swim

Fishes swim in water clear,
Birds fly up into the air,
Serpents creep along the ground,
Boys and girls run around and around.

Feathers

Cackle, cackle, Mother Goose,
Have you any feathers loose?
Truly have I, pretty fellow,
Half enough to fill a pillow.
Here are quills, take one or two,
And down to make a bed for you.

Cut Thistles

Cut thistles in May,
They'll grow in a day;
Cut them in June,
That is too soon;
Cut them in July,
Then they will die.

Pussycat and Robin

Little Robin Redbreast sat upon a tree,
Up went pussycat, and down went he!
Down came pussycat, and away Robin ran;
Says little Robin Redbreast,
"Catch me if you can!"

Robin and Pussycat

Little Robin Redbreast jumped upon a wall,
Pussycat jumped after him,
And almost had a fall!
Little Robin chirped and sang,
And what did pussycat say?
Pussycat said, "Meow,"
And Robin jumped away.

Three Blind Mice

Three blind mice, three blind mice!
See how they run, see how they run!
They all ran after the farmer's wife,
Who cut off their tails with a carving knife,
Did ever you see such a thing in your life,
As three blind mice?

Bedtime

The evening is coming, the sun sinks to rest;
The rooks are all flying straight home to the nest.
"Caw!" says the rook, as he flies overhead;
"It's time little people were going to bed!"

The flowers are closing; the daisy's asleep;
The primrose is buried in slumber so deep.
Shut up for the night is the Pimpernel red;
It's time little people were going to bed!

The butterfly, drowsy, has folded its wing;
The bees are returning, no more the birds sing.
Their labor is over, their nestlings are fed;
It's time little people were going to bed!

Hush, Little Baby

Hush, little baby, don't say a word,
Papa's gonna buy you a mockingbird.

If that mockingbird don't sing,
Papa's gonna buy you a diamond ring.

If that diamond ring turns brass,
Papa's gonna buy you a looking glass.

If that looking glass gets broke,
Papa's gonna buy you a billy goat.

If that billy goat don't pull,
Papa's gonna buy you a cart and bull.

If that cart and bull turn over,
Papa's gonna buy you a dog named Rover.

And if that dog named Rover won't bark.
Papa's gonna to buy you and horse and cart.

And if that horse and cart fall down,
You'll still be the sweetest little baby in town.

The Case of the Disappearing Books

It was the hottest summer Molly could remember. She'd walked to the libary on an errand for her mom.

"I'd like a book about baking cakes," she told Miss Brown, the librarian.

Miss Brown shook her head. "Sorry, Molly. A lot of the books have disappeared." She pointed to a big gap on a shelf.

"All the books in the library have disappeared!" said Molly, when she got home.

"Never mind," said Molly's mom. "It's too hot to cook anyway." She gave Molly a cool drink. "Your friend Lauren

phoned and she's invited you over to her house this afternoon."

"Oh, great!" Molly said, forgetting all about the missing books.

Lauren lived in a big house just outside the town. Her dad was Freddy Parker—he had been a famous rock star a long time ago.

When Molly arrived

198

at Lauren's house, Lauren's dad was complaining about the hot weather. All the doors in the house were open to keep the rooms cool. Molly's eyes widened as she saw that they were wedged open with books.

She opened one. It was a library book. Molly looked around. At least fifty library books were propping open the doors!

"Look, Lauren," she whispered.

Lauren turned to her dad. "Daddy! You can't take this many books from the library, just because you're famous!" she scolded.

"I guess you're right, Lauren," Freddy said. "Let's take the books back."

Freddy, Lauren and Molly staggered into the library carrying armfuls of books.

"Hey, sorry I borrowed your books without asking," Freddy said to Miss Brown. "Why don't you come over for a swim?" He gave Miss Brown his famous smile.

Miss Brown was very pleased to get her books back. But she was even more pleased to meet her favorite rock star.

An hour or so later, Miss Brown was sipping a cool drink with Freddy, as Molly and Lauren splashed about in the Parkers' pool.

"This is the life!" Molly heard her say.

Perfect Pony

Pepper thought that he was the luckiest pony on the whole of Merrymead Farm. He wasn't the most handsome, the smartest, or even the fastest pony but Pepper didn't mind one bit. He knew he was the luckiest pony on the farm because Jessica owned him.

Jessica was never cross or mean and always took Pepper for the nicest of rides. She ignored the other children and their ponies when they laughed at Pepper for knocking down the odd jump or for going slower than everyone else.

"They're just jealous," she'd whisper. "Because you're the best pony on the whole farm." And most of the time, Pepper managed to believe her. After all, Jessica was always right.

One summer evening, Jessica rushed out to the meadow with a piece of paper in her hand.

"Look, Pepper," she cried. "There's going to be a horse show tomorrow right here on Merrymead Farm! There are going to be games and jumping and even a showing class. I can't wait. I know that we're going to win a lot of lovely rosettes."

As Jessica rushed off to spread the news, the other ponies in the meadow started to snicker.

"Oh dear!" laughed Bluey, the largest of the ponies. "I don't think you're built for jumping."

"Your legs are too short to go fast," said Swallow, the quickest pony on the farm.

"You're far too scruffy for showing," said Ebony, the sleek and vain show pony.

That night, Pepper lay awake worrying about the horse show. "The other ponies are right," he thought. "I'm no good for anything. I'm bound to let Jessica down at the horse show."

As these thoughts tumbled through his head, Pepper fell into a restless, dream-filled sleep. He dreamed that a beautiful white horse appeared before him. "I am the Great White Horse," she whispered. "I've come to help you."

Pepper blinked as she called, "Fly with me to see the best pony on Merrymead Farm."

Pepper felt his hoofs lift from the ground.

"*Whooaah*," he cried, waggling his legs as he soared through the sky.

"Now look below you," said the Great White Horse.

Pepper looked down on a familiar scene. "It's the farm," he cried. "And look, Jessica and I are trotting past the geese."

"Yes, and look at all the other ponies," said the Great White Horse. "While you march past the geese without any fuss, they shake with fear or run away."

The Great White Horse reared up and tossed her flowing mane and the scene beneath them changed.

Pepper watched as the children got their ponies ready for a ride. He couldn't help smiling as he watched himself and Jessica rubbing noses. That was one of their favorite games.

Behind Jessica, Pepper could see Bluey putting back his ears and waving his back leg at his little boy.

"Ooh! That's not nice," gasped Pepper.

"Exactly," said the Great White Horse. "Pepper, you are brave, loyal, and kind. You are the perfect pony for Jessica. Just be yourself tomorrow and everything will be all right!"

In the horse show the next day, the first class was the jumping. Pepper set off at a steady trot. Slowly but surely he sailed clear over each jump.

"Nearly there," he thought, as he launched himself at the last jump. But his back hoof tapped the pole and it rattled to the ground. Pepper couldn't believe his bad luck. But Jessica was delighted, particularly when she was given a red rosette for coming fourth.

In the egg and spoon race, Pepper trotted so steadily that Jessica didn't drop her egg once. Jessica was over the moon when they were given a yellow rosette for coming third.

And they did even better in the pole-bending race, even though Pepper's round belly made it difficult to bend quickly round the poles.

"Well done," said the judge, as she awarded Pepper a beautiful blue rosette for coming second.

The final event of the day was the showing class.

"All the other ponies are smarter than me," thought Pepper. But as he trotted around, he remembered the words of the Great White Horse and began to relax. He was so busy enjoying himself that it took a few seconds to realize that the judge was saying something.

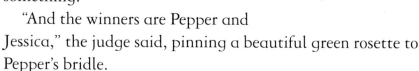

"And the winners are Pepper and Jessica," the judge said, pinning a beautiful green rosette to Pepper's bridle.

Jessica laughed in delight and rubbed noses with Pepper.

Pepper gasped. Then he looked up at the sky.

"Thank you, Great White Horse," he whispered.

Oranges and Lemons

Oranges and lemons
Say the bells of St. Clements.
I owe you five farthings
Say the bells of St. Martins.
When will you pay me?
Say the bells of Old Bailey.
When I grow rich
Say the bells of Shoreditch.

London Bells

Gay go up and gay go down,
To ring the bells of London town.
Halfpence and farthings
Say the bells of St. Martin's.
Pancakes and fritters
Say the bells of St. Peter's.
Two sticks and an apple
Say the bells of Whitechapel.

My Little Cow

I had a little cow,
Hey diddle, ho diddle!
I had a little cow, and I drove it to the stall;
Hey diddle, ho diddle! And there's my song all.

Jemmy Dawson

Brave news is come to town,
Brave news is carried;
Brave news is come to town,
Jemmy Dawson's married.

I See the Moon

I see the moon,
And the moon sees me;
God bless the moon,
And God bless me.

For Every Evil Under the Sun

For every evil under the sun,
There is a remedy, or there is none.
If there be one, try and find it;
If there be none, never mind it.

Juanita's Big Chance

The Starlight Ballet School was putting on a show.

Juanita wanted to dance in the show, so she tried very hard to dance well in class. She concentrated as hard as she could and she practiced her ballet steps at home every single night.

Miss Silver was delighted with the way Juanita had been dancing.

"I'm going to give you the role of the fairy queen, Juanita," she said, giving Juanita a pink and yellow dress.

Juanita looked at the dress. It looked very big. But she didn't say anything to Miss Silver because she wanted to be the fairy queen more than anything in the world.

When Juanita tried on the dress at home her worst fears were realized. It was much too big!

"Oh, no!" thought Juanita. She was worried. She was worried that Miss Silver might give the part to a bigger girl.

Just then Juanita's mom called her for dinner.

"Coming, Mom!" said Juanita. She took off her dress and went downstairs.

"Where's your dress, Juanita?" asked Miss Silver at the next ballet class, when they were rehearsing for the show.

"I forgot it, Miss Silver," said Juanita.

Her face felt hot and red.

"Just make sure you don't forget it for the show," said Miss Silver. Juanita looked down. She felt very bad. The dress was too big and she knew that she had told a lie.

On the way home, Juanita knew what she must do. "I will tell Mom," she thought.

"Mom, I need to..." she said, as soon as she got home. But before she could continue Mom interrupted her.

"Juanita, I'm so sorry. Your lovely dress has shrunk in the laundry!" she said.

Juanita smiled to herself. She went upstairs and tried on the dress again.

It was the perfect fit!

Let's Play!

Molly wanted to play.

"Let's play, Hetty," said Molly.

"Not today, Molly," said Hetty the horse.

"But it's so nice and sunny, Hetty," said Molly. "Perfect weather for playing!"

"Not today, Molly," said Hetty.

"I have a new ball!" said Molly to Hetty. "All the more reason to play. Come on!"

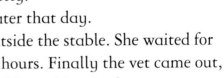

"Not today, Molly," said Hetty.

The vet came to see Hetty later that day.

Molly waited and waited outside the stable. She waited for hours. Finally the vet came out, followed by the farmer.

Then Hetty came out. But behind her Molly could see someone else. It was a new foal!

"This is Twinkle," said Hetty proudly.

"Hello, Twinkle," said Molly.

"Hello, Molly," said Twinkle.

"Now we can all play together!" said Hetty.

This Is Fun!

Chucky the hen was in the barn sitting on her egg. She sighed to herself. "Sitting on eggs is boring," she thought.

Then Dotty the duck waddled past.

"I'm going to the pond to swim," said Dotty. "Come along!"

"Okay!" said Chucky.

At the pond, Dotty swam in circles. "This is fun!" she said.

"Now or never," thought Chucky. She jumped in. It was freezing! It was wet! There was slimy green duckweed everywhere!

Chucky had forgotten that ducks are designed for swimming on ponds. They have warm, waterproof feathers and webbed feet and they like slimy green duckweed.

Hens are not designed for swimming on ponds.

Chucky coughed and spluttered and flapped her wings. Finally she managed to scramble out of the pond.

"I'm going home," she shivered.

Chucky sat on her egg. The barn was lovely and warm.

"Now this is fun!" clucked Chucky.

Twinkle, Twinkle

Twinkle, twinkle, little star,
How I wonder what you are!
Up above the world so high,
Like a diamond in the sky.

When the blazing sun is gone,
When he nothing shines upon,
Then you show your little light,
Twinkle, twinkle, all the night.

Then the traveler in the dark,
Thanks you for your tiny spark,
He could not see which way to go,
If you did not twinkle so.

As your bright and tiny spark,
Lights the traveler in the dark—
Though I know not what you are,
Twinkle, twinkle, little star.

Sleep, Baby, Sleep

Sleep, baby, sleep,
Your father keeps the sheep;
Your mother shakes the dreamland tree
And from it fall sweet dreams for thee;
Sleep, baby, sleep.

Sleep, baby, sleep,
The large stars are the sheep;
The little stars are the lambs, I guess,
And the gentle moon is the shepherdess;
Sleep, baby, sleep.

Sleep, baby, sleep,
Your father keeps the sheep;
Your mother guards the lambs this night,
And keeps them safe till morning light;
Sleep, baby, sleep.

My Best Friend

Emily was playing in the backyard with her favorite doll, Hannah.

"Hello, Emily!" called a cheerful voice.

It was Sarah, who lived next door. The two girls were best friends.

"Can I play with Hannah, too?" asked Sarah, reaching out to pick her up.

Emily held on tightly to Hannah. She was a very special doll, and Emily didn't like anybody else to play with her.

"Hannah's tired," said Emily. "I think I'll put her to bed. Then I'll come back and play with you."

For the rest of the morning, Emily and Sarah played in Emily's treehouse. It was their special hideout, and nobody else was allowed in it.

They both thought it was great living next door to one another.

The next day, both girls got up early and ran down to the front garden. They were very excited. They were going on vacation together. Every year, they went to the same vacation resort. Sarah was traveling with Emily's family. That way they could talk to each other on the journey.

"Can Hannah sit between us?" Sarah asked Emily as they climbed into the car.

"Sorry," said Emily. "Hannah says she wants to sit by the window." And she tucked Hannah safely out of Sarah's reach.

At last they arrived at the house, and the girls raced from room to room checking that nothing had changed since last year. At bedtime, they snuggled down in their cozy beds in the attic. They loved sharing a room on vacation. They stayed awake long after the lights went out, talking and laughing together.

This vacation was the best one yet. One day Sarah rode her bicycle without training wheels for the first time. The next day Emily did the same. Soon the girls were racing each other.

"Can we keep on racing each other when we get home?" Sarah asked her mom and dad. Her mom frowned.

"Hmmm," she began. "There's something we've been meaning to tell you. We're moving away. Daddy's got a new job, and we've found a wonderful new house."

Emily and Sarah couldn't believe their ears. They wouldn't be neighbors anymore!

"It's not too far. You'll still be able to see Emily on weekends and during vacations," Dad said.

"But I don't want to move!" cried Sarah. She threw her arms around Emily. "You won't forget me, will you?" she whispered.

Back at home after the vacation, the last days of the summer flew by. On the morning that Sarah and her family were due to leave, Emily and her parents came outside to say good-bye.

"I've brought you a present to remember me by," said Sarah, handing Emily the gift. Emily ripped off the paper. Nestled inside was a gorgeous golden heart necklace.

"It's beautiful!" Emily smiled. Then she rushed inside her house. She came out a minute later carrying Hannah.

"Here," she said, putting the doll into Sarah's arms. "Hannah will keep you company until you make friends at your new house."

Sarah was speechless. She gave Emily an enormous hug.

Emily grinned. "Sharing really is great," she declared. "Especially sharing things with your very best friend."

Frère Jacques

Frère Jacques, Frère Jacques,
Dormez-vous, dormez-vous?
Sonnez les matines, sonnez les matines,
Ding, dang, dong, ding, dang, dong.

O Lady Moon

O Lady Moon, your horns point toward the east—
Shine, be increased.
O Lady Moon, your horns point toward the west—
Wane, be at rest.

Ding, Dong, Bell

Ding, dong, bell,
Pussy's in the well!
Who put her in?
Little Tommy Green.
Who pulled her out?
Little Johnny Stout.
What a naughty boy was that
To try to drown poor pussycat,
Who never did any harm,
But killed the mice in his father's barn.

Muffin Man

Have you seen the muffin man,
The muffin man, the muffin man,
Have you seen the muffin man
That lives in Drury Lane, oh?

The Coachman

Up at Piccadilly, oh!
The coachman takes his stand,
And when he meets a pretty girl,
He takes her by the hand;
Whip away for ever, oh!
Drive away so clever, oh!
All the way to Bristol, oh!
He drives her four-in-hand.

The Miller of Dee

There was a jolly miller
Lived on the river Dee:
He worked and sang from morn 'til night,
No lark so blithe as he;
And this the burden of his song for ever used to be—
I jump me jerrime jee!
I care for nobody—no! not I,
Since nobody cares for me.

The Case of the Disgusting Doughnuts

"One doughnut, please," Molly said. She handed her money to Mr. Jones, the baker. Mr. Jones made the best doughnuts ever.

Molly sat down on a bench outside the bakery. She took a great big bite out of her doughnut. "Yuk!" she said, spitting it out. It tasted disgusting.

Lauren and Carlos, two of Molly's school friends, walked by. "You're eating one of Mr. Jones's doughnuts, aren't you?" Carlos asked. "They used to be delicious, but not any more. We've stopped buying them."

"I don't blame you," said Molly, throwing the rest of her doughnut in the garbage can. She heard giggling and turned around. It was John and Jamie, Mr. Jones's twin sons.

"What's so funny?" Molly asked angrily.

"Nothing," they said. They ran quickly back into the bakery, still giggling.

"I wonder if the twins are somehow behind the disgusting doughnuts?" said Molly thoughtfully.

"I bet they are!" Lauren replied. "Do you remember when they watered down all the glue at school so it wouldn't stick?"

"Let's find out!" said Carlos.

The three friends crept into the bakery. John and Jamie were in the kitchen.

"Look what they're doing!" whispered Molly. John and

Jamie were pouring salt into their dad's sugar shaker.

So this was what had happened to Mr. Jones's doughnuts! He was sweetening them with salt instead of sugar.

Molly grabbed hold of John and Jamie and dragged them into the store. John was still holding the sugar shaker. Jamie was pretending to cry.

"Look what John and Jamie have been doing, Mr. Jones!" said Molly. "They've been putting salt on your doughnuts and ruining them."

Mr. Jones was very annoyed. "You two can spend the weekend cleaning the kitchen," he said.

Then he turned to Molly, Lauren and Carlos. "Thank you! You can each take home a free box of cakes," he said, smiling. "But I'll understand if you don't choose doughnuts!"

Mia's Star Surprise

Mia had a lot of ballet posters on her bedroom walls. They all showed her favorite ballet star—Ana Jones.

Ana Jones had learned to dance at the Starlight Ballet School.

"I want to dance like Ana Jones when I grow up," said Mia to her mom.

"She went to your ballet school," said her mom.

"I know," said Mia.

A few days later Mia and her mom and dad arrived at the Starlight Ballet School for Mia's class.

They arrived at the same time as a lady on her own.

Just as the lady was going into the ballet school she dropped her keys.

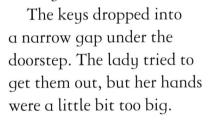

The keys dropped into a narrow gap under the doorstep. The lady tried to get them out, but her hands were a little bit too big.

Mia ran over to help. Her hands were small enough to reach into the gap. She fished out the keys and gave them to the lady.

The lady turned to Mia. "Thank you," she said.

Mia gasped.

It was Ana Jones!

"Are you going to your dance class?" said Ana Jones.

Mia nodded. She couldn't speak.

"Miss Silver asked me to teach your class today," smiled Ana.

"Wow!" said Mia.

"Look! It's Ana Jones! She's talking to Mia!" said Mia's friends.

All the students got dressed quickly.

Ana Jones took the class while Miss Silver sat and watched.

Ana was the most graceful ballerina Mia had ever seen. Mia watched Ana closely and tried to move like she did.

"Well done, Mia!" cried Ana, when Mia did a beautiful arabesque. "That was lovely."

Mia had never been able to do an arabesque well before. She couldn't stop smiling as she danced.

"What did you think of the class?" her mom asked at the end of the lesson.

"It was the best class ever!" said Mia.

Molly Mouse

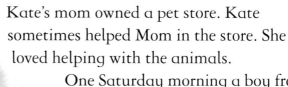

Kate's mom owned a pet store. Kate sometimes helped Mom in the store. She loved helping with the animals.

One Saturday morning a boy from Kate's school called Jim came to buy a mouse. He picked a gray mouse.

"I will call her Molly," said Jim, stroking the mouse. Molly squeaked.

"Hello, Molly," said Kate.

Just then the door opened and a woman came in with a dog. The dog barked loudly when he saw all the other animals in the pet store.

Molly squeaked and jumped out of Jim's hands.

"Oh, no!" said Kate. "Where are you, Molly?"

They looked under the table. Molly wasn't there.

They looked behind the counter. Molly wasn't there.

They looked under the cash register. Molly wasn't there.

Finally, Kate and Jim looked in the mouse cage. And Molly was there!

"What a sensible mouse!" said Kate's mom.

Molly was happy to see Jim. She ran over to him, squeaking happily.

"And it looks like she already knows who owns her," said Kate.

Tiger

Three kittens were in Kate's mom's pet store. One kitten was black and white. One kitten was pure white. One kitten was orange and stripy like a tiger. Kate liked the orange kitten best.

A family came into the store after school one day.

"Which kitten do you want?" the mom said to the little girl.

"I like the black-and-white kitten best," said the little girl, stroking him. So they took the black-and-white kitten home.

A few days later a woman came into the store.

"How cute!" she cried when she saw the white kitten's fluffy fur. So she took the white kitten home.

Days went by. No one picked the orange kitten. Kate played with him. She thought he missed his brother and sister.

Mom watched Kate playing with the kitten.

"Would you like to have that kitten, Kate?" she said.

"Really?" said Kate. She had never had a pet of her own.

"Really," said Mom. Kate laughed. The kitten purred.

"I will call him Tiger," said Kate.

Now the Day Is Over

Now the day is over,
Night is drawing nigh,
Shadows of evening
Steal across the sky.

Now the darkness gathers,
Stars begin to peep,
Birds and beasts and flowers
Soon will be asleep.

I Saw a Ship

I saw a ship a-sailing,
A-sailing on the sea;
And, oh! it was all laden
With pretty things for thee!

There were comfits in the cabin,
And apples in the hold
The sails were made of silk,
And the masts were made of gold.

The four-and-twenty sailors
That stood between the decks,
Were four-and-twenty white mice
With chains about their necks.

The captain was a duck,
With a packet on his back;
And when the ship began to move,
The captain said, "Quack! Quack!"

Fairer Princess Sarah

Sarah was the fairest royal princess in the land,
And every prince for miles around longed to win her hand.
But though she was a picture—the loveliest you've seen—
Sarah had another side. She could be *really* mean!

She wouldn't even let her friends touch her things, you see.
"Hands off my pretty toys," she'd shout. "They all belong to me!
Leave my precious jewels alone... and *please* don't touch my dress!
You'll just get it dirty and make a horrid mess!"

Her friends grew quickly fed up: "Just keep your silly old stuff.
We don't want to play with you. This time we've had enough!"
"How dare they speak to me like that!"cried Sarah in surprise.
She ran off to the woods to sulk, tears filling up her eyes.

Then Sarah heard a gentle voice. "There is no need to cry!
Every problem can be solved," said thoughtful Sir MacEye.
"Though your eyes are like stars, and although you may be fair...
A kindly heart means so much more, so why not try to share?"

Sarah listened to his words. "How wise you are," she said.
"I don't need so many things, so I'll share them instead.
For though I love pretty things and clothes that make me fairer,
I'd rather share with my friends, and just be plain old Sarah!"

Where Are You Going to, My Pretty Maid?

Where are you going to, my pretty maid?
Where are you going to, my pretty maid?
I'm going a-milking, sir, she said,
Sir, she said, sir, she said,
I'm going a-milking, sir, she said.

May I go with you, my pretty maid?
May I go with you, my pretty maid?
You're kindly welcome, sir, she said,
Sir, she said, sir, she said,
You're kindly welcome, sir, she said.

What is your fortune, my pretty maid?
What is your fortune, my pretty maid?
My face is my fortune, sir, she said,
Sir, she said, sir, she said,
My face is my fortune, sir, she said.

Then I can't marry you, my pretty maid,
Then I can't marry you, my pretty maid,
Nobody asked you, sir, she said,
Sir, she said, sir, she said,
Nobody asked you, sir, she said.

Monday's Child

Monday's child is fair of face,
Tuesday's child is full of grace,
Wednesday's child is full of woe,
Thursday's child has far to go,
Friday's child is loving and giving,
Saturday's child works hard for his living,
And the child that is born on the Sabbath day
Is bonny and blithe, and good, and gay.

The Case of the Ghost in the Attic

Molly was doing her homework with Carlos one evening when there was a knock at the front door. It was Mrs. Dimley, the next-door neighbor. She looked a bit frightened.

"Is anything the matter?" asked Molly's mom.

"I think my house is haunted!" Mrs. Dimley replied.

Molly grew excited. She loved ghost stories.

"At night, I can hear bumping coming from my attic," explained Mrs. Dimley.

Molly's mom made everyone a nice cup of tea, and Mrs. Dimley said she felt better.

But next evening Mrs. Dimley came back looking upset. "My lights aren't working now, and the TV keeps going on and off," she said. "If this doesn't stop, I'll have to move away!"

Molly didn't want her to leave. It was time to investigate!

"Mom, can we borrow a flashlight?" she asked. "We're going next door to look in Mrs. Dimley's attic."

"I'll come with you," said her dad.

Molly's dad helped her and Carlos up into Mrs. Dimley's attic. When Molly switched on her flashlight, she couldn't believe her eyes. What a mess! There were shredded newspapers everywhere. Hiding in a corner there was a family of frightened squirrels.

"Dad!" called Molly. "Look what we've found!"

Her dad climbed up the ladder and looked into the attic. "Those squirrels must have got in through that hole in the roof," he chuckled. "They've chewed through a lot of wires. No wonder Mrs. Dimley's electricity isn't working properly!"

Carlos ran next door to tell Mrs. Dimley the news.

"Thank goodness for that!" she said. She phoned her friend who was a vet and he came round straight away.

"I'll take your squirrels to the local park," he said.

"And I'll mend the hole in your roof," said Molly's dad.

Mrs. Dimley was pleased. "You're all so kind," she said. She gave Molly and Carlos a big hug. "And you two are very clever kids!"

Star Light, Star Bright

Star light, star bright,
First star I see tonight,
I wish I may, I wish I might,
Have the wish I wish tonight.

Little Cottage

Little cottage in the wood,
Little old man by the window stood,
Saw a rabbit running by,
Knocking at the door.
"Help me! Help me! Help me!" he said,
"Before the huntsman shoots me dead."
"Come little rabbit, come inside,
Safe with me abide."

Here Is the Church

Here is the church,
Here is the steeple,
Open the doors,
And here are the people.
Here is the parson, going upstairs,
And here he is a-saying his prayers.

How Many Miles to Babylon?

How many miles to Babylon?—
Threescore and ten.
Can I get there by candlelight?—
Aye, and back again!

A Swarm of Bees in May

A swarm of bees in May
Is worth a load of hay;
A swarm of bees in June
Is worth a silver spoon;
A swarm of bees in July
Is not worth a fly.

Tinker, Tailor

Tinker, tailor,
Soldier, sailor,
Rich man, poor man,
Beggarman, thief!

Kylee in the Spotlight

It was show night at the Starlight Ballet School, but Kylee had hurt her foot while riding her bike the day before. She wouldn't be able to dance in the show.

On the way to watch the show, Kylee's mom tried to cheer her up.

"You'll be in the next show," she said.

"But not this show," said Kylee, with a sniff.

When they got to the Starlight Ballet School Kylee went backstage to wish her friends luck.

"Good luck, Juanita," said Kylee.

Juanita gave Kylee a big hug. "I wish you could be in the show, too," she said.

Just then Miss Silver came into the room. She looked worried. "Has anyone seen the clown doll?" she asked.

"No," said everyone.

"Oh dear!" said Miss Silver. "I think it's lost!"

The clown doll was very important because the dancers danced around it during the big dance at the end of the show.

"We won't be able to do the clown dance," said Juanita.

"The show will be ruined!" cried Mia.

Kylee looked at all the costumes hanging on the wall. There was an old clown costume hanging there that had been used for a show the previous year.

Kylee had an idea.

"Miss Silver, I could dress up as the clown doll," she said.

"Thank you, Kylee!" said Miss Silver. "What a good idea. You have saved the day."

Kylee raced out to tell her parents what had happened and then put on the clown costume.

At the end of the show all the dancers gathered on stage.

"And we'd like to give special thanks to Kylee for her quick thinking," said Miss Silver. "She really saved the show."

Everyone applauded. Kylee smiled broadly. She had got to be in the show after all!

The Midnight Fairies

Megan was staying with Grandma for a few days, while Mom was away.

Megan always had fun at Grandma's. But on the second night of Megan's visit, as she was getting ready for bed, Megan realized that she'd lost the pretty flower necklace Mom had given her. Megan and Grandma looked everywhere, but they couldn't find it.

Grandma gave Megan a hug. "Don't worry. We'll look in the backyard tomorrow," she promised. "I'm sure it will be there."

Megan settled down to sleep, but she tossed and turned and finally woke up again. She couldn't stop thinking about her lost necklace.

Getting out of bed, she went to look out of the window. Somewhere in the distance, a clock chimed once...twice... twelve times. "Midnight!" Megan thought. Suddenly her eyes opened wide. At the end of the moonlit backyard, where the wild flowers grew, lights began to wink and twinkle, and shimmering shapes danced in the air.

Fairies had come out to play! They danced and skipped through the air, laughing and flitting from flower to flower.

All at once Fairy Firefly saw something—a silver necklace gleaming in the grass.

"Look!" she said to her fairy friends.

"I wonder who this belongs to!"

"Maybe it's that little girl's," said Nightingale, pointing up to the window where Megan was looking out. "She looks very sad—as if she's lost something special."

"I wish we could make her smile again," said Moon Blossom.

The fairies looked at one another, and knew they were all thinking the same thing. First, they tucked the necklace safely behind a stone. Then, together, they flew across the backyard and straight up to Megan's window.

As Megan gasped with amazement and delight, Stardust sprinkled her with glittering fairy dust.

"Now you'll be able to fly with us!" the fairies said happily.

With a fairy holding each hand, Megan whooshed out of the window and flew down to the end of the backyard. When they landed, Stardust introduced herself and her friends. "We are the Midnight Fairies," she explained. "Every night at midnight, we come out to dance and play in the moonlight.

Will you be our friend and play with us tonight?"

"Of course I will!" said Megan happily.

With the moon beaming down and the friendly stars twinkling above, Megan and the fairies danced among the wild flowers. The cool grass tickled Megan's toes, and the fairies' laughter sounded like tiny crystal bells. Megan laughed with them, and felt happier than she ever had before.

When Megan was too tired to dance anymore, Firefly said, "We have a surprise for you." She brought out Megan's necklace.

"My necklace!" cried Megan. "You found it! Thank you!"

As Firefly gave the necklace back, Stardust sprinkled magic fairy dust over it. A beautiful fairy appeared in place of the flower.

"Oh!" breathed Megan. "How wonderful. It's you! It's a Midnight Fairy!"

"Yes," said Firefly. "But please
don't tell anyone how it got
there, or we might lose our
fairy magic."

"I promise!" replied
Megan.

As she put on her

necklace, Megan realized that she could barely keep her eyes open. With the Midnight Fairies fluttering over her, she curled up under the oak tree and fell asleep...until the morning, when she woke up, tucked up in her cozy bed in Grandma's house!

"How did I get back here?" Megan wondered. "Was it just a dream?"

She reached up to her neck—and there was her necklace, right where it should be.

"Good morning!" said Grandma cheerfully, opening the bedroom door.

"Grandma, look!" said Megan. "I have my necklace back! Did *you* find it?"

"No, dear," said Grandma, with a puzzled look. She peered down at the necklace. "Oh, how lovely!" she said. "I hadn't noticed the fairy before."

"The Midnight Fairies!" Megan thought to herself. "So it wasn't a dream, after all!"

"I wonder how your necklace got back here," said Grandma, scratching her head.

Megan, smiling as she looked out toward the backyard, knew the answer. But it was a secret that belonged to her—to her and the Midnight Fairies, the wonderful, magical friends she would never, ever forget.

Fudge Won't Play

Sam had a pet hamster. Her name was Fudge.

Sam's sister Sophie wanted to play with Fudge.

"Fudge won't play," said Sam. "She's hiding."

Sophie looked in Fudge's cage. The hamster was curled up inside her nest.

Mom looked at Fudge. "Fudge is getting very plump," she said. "We will take her to the vet."

Sam, Sophie, and Mom went in the car to the vet. The vet picked up Fudge and looked at her.

"Is Fudge ill?" said Sam.

The vet smiled. "No," she said, stroking Fudge. "Fudge is going to have babies."

"Can we keep all the babies?" asked Sophie.

"We'll see," said Mom.

Sam put Fudge back in her cage and they went home in the car.

All the way back they talked excitedly about Fudge's babies.

"I wonder how many babies Fudge will have," said Sophie.

"I wonder what color they will be," said Sam.

"Dad will be surprised, won't he?" said Sophie.

"He certainly will!" said Mom.

Sam held Fudge's cage carefully all the way home. But the three of them were so busy talking about Fudge's babies that they didn't notice the door of the cage wasn't closed properly.

At home, Dad went to look at Fudge. He came back with a frown on his face.

"Fudge isn't in her cage," said Dad.

Sam and Sophie raced upstairs. The cage door was open.

"Fudge is missing!" said Sam.

"What will happen to her babies?" said Sophie.

"Don't panic," said Mom. "I'm sure we'll find her. Sophie, you look upstairs. Sam, you go and look in the car."

Sam ran out to look in the car. A minute later he came racing back in with a big smile on his face. "I found her," he said. "And there's a surprise in the car, too!"

They went to look in the car.

"Here she is!" said Sam.

Fudge was on the back seat. And so were all her babies!

241

Lost Billy

Kate and her mom were walking in the park when a dog started to follow them.

"Woof!" barked the dog mournfully. Kate looked at him.

"He looks lost," she said.

Mom bent down to pat him. "He does," she agreed. "But he doesn't have a collar, so we don't know who he belongs to."

Kate's mom took the dog back to her pet store. She put a sign in the window saying that they had found a brown-and-white dog with black ears and a black tail.

A few days later a boy came into the pet store. As soon as he walked through the door the dog started barking excitedly. He jumped up and started licking the boy's face.

"Billy!" said the boy, with a big smile on his face.

"Woof!" barked Billy happily, jumping all around Jamal.

"My name's Jamal," said the boy. "Billy is my dog."

Jamal put a new collar on Billy. "Now Billy won't get lost," he said.

Kate was sad. "I will miss Billy," she said.

"Come and play with us whenever you want," said Jamal.

"OK!" said Kate, smiling. She had two new friends!

Pretty Polly

It was Mom's birthday. Kate wanted to get her a present.

"What do you think I should get Mom?" she asked Jamal.

"Maybe a bag," said Jamal.

"Maybe a bag," squawked Polly Parrot.

Kate shook her head.

"Maybe a mug," said Jamal.

"Maybe a mug," said Polly.

Kate shook her head.

"Maybe a hat," said Jamal.

"Maybe a hat," said Polly.

"Good idea!" said Kate.

Kate and Jamal and Jamal's mom went to the hat store. They picked out a hat for Mom. They wrapped it in paper and tied it with a ribbon.

Kate gave Mom the present.

"I wonder what it is?" Mom said.

"Maybe a bag," squawked Polly Parrot.

"Shhh, Polly," said Kate. Mom took off the ribbon.

"Maybe a mug," said Polly.

"Shhh, Polly," said Kate. Mom took off the paper.

"Maybe a hat!" said Polly.

"What a pretty hat," said Mom.

"What a pretty hat," squawked Polly.

Here We Go Round the Mulberry Bush

Here we go round the mulberry bush,
The mulberry bush, the mulberry bush,
Here we go round the mulberry bush,
On a cold and frosty morning.

This is the way we wash our hands,
Wash our hands, wash our hands,
This is the way we wash our hands,
On a cold and frosty morning.

This is the way we wash our clothes,
Wash our clothes, wash our clothes,
This is the way we wash our clothes,
On a cold and frosty morning.

Here we go round the mulberry bush,
The mulberry bush, the mulberry bush,
Here we go round the mulberry bush,
On a cold and frosty morning.

Lavender's Blue

Lavender's blue,
Dilly, dilly,
Lavender's green,
When I am king,
Dilly, dilly,
You shall be queen.

Call up your men,
Dilly, dilly,
Set them to work,
Some to the plow,
Dilly, dilly,
Some to the cart;

Some to make hay,
Dilly, dilly,
Some to thresh corn;
Whilst you and I,
Dilly, dilly,
Keep ourselves warm.

Itsy Bitsy Spider

Itsy Bitsy spider
Climbing up the spout;
Down came the rain
And washed the spider out.
Out came the sunshine
And dried up all the rain;
Itsy Bitsy spider
Climbed up the spout again.

Bow, Wow, Wow

Bow, wow, wow,
Whose dog art thou?
"Little Tom Tinker's dog,
Bow, wow, wow."

The Cold Old House

I know a house, and a cold old house,
A cold old house by the sea.
If I were a mouse in that cold old house
What a cold, cold mouse I'd be!

Hickory, Dickory, Dock

Hickory, dickory, dock,
The mouse ran up the clock.
The clock struck one,
The mouse ran down,
Hickory, dickory, dock.

Bat, Bat

Bat, bat, come under my hat,
And I'll give you a slice of bacon,
And when I bake I'll give you a cake,
If I am not mistaken.

Little Jack Horner

Little Jack Horner,
Sat in a corner,
Eating a Christmas pie.
He put in his thumb,
And pulled out a plum,
And said, "What a good boy am I!"

Twinkle the Tooth Fairy

Twinkle the Tooth Fairy was
always very busy. Every night, she
collected the milk teeth that the
children left under their pillows.
But the teeth were so tiny they
were difficult to find in the dark.

Late one summer's evening,
Twinkle was looking for the last
milk tooth of the night. Finally,
she found it and put her last shiny
coin under the pillow.

"Good night," whispered
Twinkle as she gently kissed the sleeping child and flew silently
out of the window. The sun was just coming up as Twinkle flew
back to Fairyland.

All the fairies in Fairyland were very busy getting ready
for the Fairy Ball. Fairy food had to be made by the best fairy
cooks. Hundreds of fairy lights had to be put up. And the fairy
orchestra was practicing very hard.

Before going to bed, Twinkle decided to go and see her friend
Thimble, the fairy dressmaker. Thimble had been busy, too,
making all the dresses for the Fairy Ball.

"What beautiful dresses!" exclaimed Twinkle.

"I'm glad you like them," said Thimble. "But they would be so much better if I could decorate them with golden thread. I can't find any in the whole of Fairyland."

"I know where there's a lot of golden thread. Leave it to me," Twinkle said excitedly, and she flew off high into the sky.

Soon, she was among hundreds of bright, shining stars. On she flew, until she reached a huge golden ball—the Sun.

"Please, Mr. Sun," she asked, "can you spare some of your fine golden thread for my friend Thimble?"

Twinkle waited. All of a sudden, a long trail of golden thread came slowly from the center of the Sun. Twinkle took the end of it, and began to pull it towards her.

"That tickles!" laughed the Sun.

Twinkle had soon gathered a large bundle of the precious thread. "Thank you, Mr. Sun," she said.

"You're very welcome, Twinkle," chuckled the Sun.

When Thimble saw what Twinkle had brought her, she clapped her hands with joy!

"Thank you, Twinkle!" she said. "Now my dresses will be perfect. And I promise you will have the finest dress of all for the ball."

"I've never been to the Fairy Ball," said Twinkle quietly.

"Why ever not?" asked Thimble, curiously.

"It takes me such a long time to

find all the children's teeth, I never get back in time," Twinkle said sadly.

"Don't you worry. I'll think of something!" said Thimble.

Twinkle felt very tired after her busy night and went straight to bed. When she woke up the next day, she was surprised to see a large bag at the foot of her bed.

Inside the bag were the most beautiful purple-and-gold velvet purses. Pinned to the bag was a note, which read:

Dear Twinkle,

I have made these special purses from the leftover fairy dress cloth. The children can put their teeth into them. The purses will be much easier for you to find in the dark. With a bit of luck, you will be back in time for the ball!

Your best fairy friend, Thimble

Later that evening, Twinkle collected all the children's milk

teeth as usual. She left each child with a shiny coin tucked into one of the purses, which she carefully placed under their pillows. Twinkle whispered to each sleeping child, "Please use the purse to keep your next milk tooth safe."

A few days later it was the night of the Fairy Ball. Twinkle was very excited. She so hoped that she'd be back in time to join in the fun! But first she had her important job to do.

When she flew off that night to collect the milk teeth, Twinkle was overjoyed to see that each child had put their milk tooth inside their purse. Now, they were easy to find!

She kissed each child and whispered, "Thank you!"

After gathering all the teeth up carefully, Twinkle flew quickly back to Fairyland. When she was nearly home, she

could hear the sounds of the fairy orchestra in the distance. The whole sky was lit up with the lights of the Fairy Ball.

"It's already started!" she thought, flying even faster.

When she reached home, Twinkle rushed to see Thimble.

"Am I too late?" she asked breathlessly.

"It's only just begun!" laughed Thimble.

Twinkle had a wonderful time at the Fairy Ball. And everyone agreed that in her beautiful new dress she was the prettiest fairy of all.

Rain, Rain, Go Away!

It was a rainy day and Raindrop the fairy liked the rain.

"Come and play outside," Raindrop said to the other fairies.

The other fairies did not like the rain. "It's too wet to play outside," they said.

All the fairies lived at the back of a yard that belonged to Ann and Tom.

Ann and Tom looked out of the window.

"I'm bored," said Ann.

"It's too wet to play outside," said Tom.

"I'm bored of being inside," said Ann.

Down at the back of the yard, Raindrop had started to cry because no one wanted to play with her. And the more Raindrop cried, the more it rained. Soon it was pouring!

Sunny the sunshine fairy looked at the rain. "Don't cry, Raindrop," she said. "I will play with you."

Raindrop stopped crying.

Like magic, the rain stopped. The sun came out.

Ann and Tom came out to play in the yard.

"Look! A beautiful rainbow!" they said.

Too Much Sun

It was a hot sunny day. Tom and Ann were too hot to play. They lay on the couch and watched television. Even the flowers in the yard were wilting in the hot sun.

"It's just too hot!" said Ann.

But Sunny the sunshine fairy, down at the back of Ann and Tom's yard, liked the sun. The hotter the better!

"Come and play in the sky," she said to her fairy friends.

Sunny, Windy, and Raindrop flew up into the sky. The fairies started to play hide-and-seek.

First of all Sunny hid in the clouds. Then Windy blew the clouds away.

Then Raindrop waved her wand at a cloud and it began to rain. She hid in the shower of rain until Windy blew the rain cloud away with a laugh.

The flowers in Ann and Tom's yard lifted up their petals gratefully when the refreshing shower of rain came down.

Now it was not too hot anymore. It was a lovely day and everything was sparkling from the shower of rain.

Tom and Ann were not too hot any more.

"Let's go and play in the yard!" said Tom.

The Case of the Stolen Necklace

"Happy birthday, Lauren!" Molly said, hugging her friend.

The birthday party began with a magic show in the garden. Everyone was amazed at the magician's clever tricks.

But then suddenly, Lauren's mom, Tracy, ran onto the stage. "Stop the show!" she cried. "I can't find my necklace!"

"Your diamond necklace?" asked Lauren's dad worriedly.

"Yes—and it's worth a fortune!" said Lauren's mom.

"Mommy's always losing her jewels and panicking," said Lauren angrily. "I bet it's not stolen at all. And it's ruined my birthday party!"

Molly wanted to help Lauren.

"I might just, er, go to the bathroom, Lauren," she said.

On the way up to the house, Molly heard a scream behind a hedge.

Behind the hedge she found Lauren's two little sisters in their playhouse. They were dressed as princesses.

"It's mine! Give it back!" said Zara.

"No, I got it first!" said Hope. She was waving a sparkly necklace in the air.

"Hello," said Molly. "Where did you get that lovely necklace?"

"We borrowed it," said Hope.

Molly laughed. "I think we'd better tell your mom," she said.

Lauren's mom was very happy to have her necklace back. "Next time, just ask before you borrow my things," she said, giving Zara and Hope a hug. "Now let's find Lauren and get this magic show started again!"

After the magic show was over, Lauren's mom made another announcement. "Good news!" she cried. "My necklace has been found. And to celebrate, all the girls are invited to try on my jewelery collection."

Lauren clapped excitedly. "Come on everyone!" she cried. "This is going to be the best birthday ever!"

Poor Peep

Sophie and Sam were playing in the yard when Miss Tring from next door came out of her house. "Peep!" she called. "Peep! Where are you?"

Peep was Miss Tring's cat.

"Is Peep missing, Miss Tring?" asked Sophie.

"Yes," said Miss Tring. "She's been missing since last night. I can't find her."

"We'll help you look for her," said Sam.

Sam and Sophie began to look. They looked all over their yard. Then Sophie heard a noise.

"What's that noise?" she said. "Where's it coming from?"

"Listen!" said Sam. The noise was coming from a big metal garbage can Sophie and Sam's dad sometimes used to keep garden waste in.

"Meow! Meow!" Sam ran to the can and opened the lid. Peep was inside. She meowed even louder.

They lifted Peep out and took her home to Miss Tring.

"She must have climbed in yesterday when Dad was working in the garden," said

Sophie to Miss Tring.

"I'm just glad she's home again," said Miss Tring.

"Meow!" meowed Peep, lifting up one of her front paws.

"Poor Peep! She has cut her paw!" said Sophie.

"We'll need to take her to the vet," said Miss Tring. "Would you like to come with me?"

"Yes, please!" said Sophie and Sam.

The vet stroked Peep. "Nothing serious, Peep," she said. "You'll soon be better." She cleaned Peep's paw and put a bandage on it.

"All better now, Peep!" said Sam, stroking her gently.

Peep began to purr.

Miss Tring smiled. "Thank you for helping!" she said.

Fairy Seasons

Spring fairies laugh and play,
Hopping and skipping
With bunnies all day.
Hop, skip, hop, skip,
To make the garden happy.
Summer fairies flutter around,
Cleaning and shining
The flowers on the ground.
Softly, softly, clean and shine,
To make the garden pretty.
Fall fairies dance around the trees,
Catching and chasing

The leaves in the breeze.
Hurry, scurry, catch the leaves,
To make the garden tidy.
Winter fairies float through the air,
Sprinkling and shaking
Snow here and there.
Gently, gently, spread the snow,
To make the garden sparkle.
Then, once a year, as a special treat,
The fairy queen and the fairies meet.
They sing and dance to celebrate
The magic in the garden.

My Mom Is Great

My mom is great.

She's brilliant at everything. I think my mom's... *magic*!

Every morning, her magic begins when she disappears into the bathroom. She changes from morning Mommy... into daytime Mommy! After that, Mom is ready to tackle anything

– even the horrible monsters that live under my bed.

Isn't my mom brave?

My mom's not afraid of anything. I'm never worried when she's around.

My mom never lets me down. She even manages to find Little Ted after I've looked everywhere—and given up hope of ever seeing him again.

Then, for her next trick, Mom mends my Mr. Wobbly.

You would never know he'd been broken.

In fact, my mom can fix

just about anything (except washing machines).

My mom always knows when I've done something wrong.

But she never stays angry with me for long.

Mom and I always have fun. Sometimes she takes me for bike rides in the country.

My mom is very smart. She always knows the answers to my questions.

And she's a fantastic cook. She makes me the yummiest meals.

My mom makes me smile when I'm sad. And she can always make me feel better with a magical hug.

Toward the end of the day Mom's magic begins to fade. By the time I'm ready for bed, she has changed back into morning Mommy.

But I don't care what Mom looks like. I don't even care if she's not really magic, because whatever she does, she's my mom and... my mom is *great*!

Happy Princess Haley

Haley was a funny kind of princess, it was thought.
She didn't always act the way a royal princess ought.
For everywhere that Haley went and every time she spoke,
She really couldn't help herself—*out* would pop a joke!

She sniggered at royal functions, and laughed aloud at school.
She giggled in the library and broke the silence rule!
But though Haley was great fun, and made her best friends smile,
She did get so annoying—laughing all the while!

"If only Haley made less noise, and played more quietly,
Instead of laughing until she bursts!" said her family.
Then one day disaster struck. Poor Haley lost her kitty.
She couldn't even raise a smile! It really was a pity.

"I wish you would laugh once more," her friends said, that night.
"Without your laughter and your jokes, the palace isn't right!
If only we could find poor Fluff and make you smile again.
If we lose your happy face, it just won't be the same!"

All at once Sir Dave appeared, in answer to their wish.
"I found this by the pond," he said, "watching all the fish!"
Princess Haley laughed out loud, to everyone's delight.
"You've found little Fluff!" she cried, kissing the blushing knight.

Now Haley's happy once again, so if they're feeling sad,
Her friends just listen to her laugh. It always makes them glad!

Polly Put the Kettle On

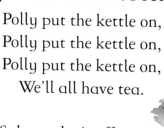

Polly put the kettle on,
Polly put the kettle on,
Polly put the kettle on,
We'll all have tea.

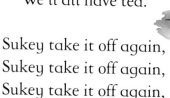

Sukey take it off again,
Sukey take it off again,
Sukey take it off again,
They've all gone away.

I Scream

I scream, you scream,
We all scream for ice cream!

A Peanut

A peanut sat on the railroad track,
His heart was all a-flutter;
Along came a train – the 9:15 –
Toot, toot, peanut butter!

Our Baby

Goodness, our baby makes a lot of noise!
He bangs his crib and throws out all his toys.
But there's one time I love to take a peep,
And that's when, finally, he falls asleep.

Pat-a-Cake

Pat-a-cake, pat-a-cake, baker's man,
Bake me a cake as fast as you can.
Pat it and prick it and mark it with B,
And put it in the oven for Baby and me.

Dibbity, Dibbity, Dibbity, Doe

Dibbity, dibbity, dibbity, doe,
Give me a pancake
And I'll go.
Dibbity, dibbity, dibbity, ditter,
Please to give me
A bit of a fritter.

Like a Duck to Water

Mrs. Duck swam proudly across the
farm pond followed by a line of fluffy
ducklings. Hidden in the safety of the
nest, Dozy Duckling peeked out and
watched them go. He wished he was
brave enough to go with them but
he was afraid of the water!

When they returned that night
they told him tales of all the scary
animals they had met by the pond.

"There's a big thing with hot breath called Horse," said Dotty.

"There's a huge smelly pink thing called Pig," said Dickie.

"But worst of all," said Doris, "there's a great gray bird
called Heron. He gobbles up little ducklings for breakfast!"

At that, all the little ducklings squawked with fear and
excitement.

Next morning, Mrs. Duck hurried the ducklings out for
their morning parade. Dozy kept his eyes shut until they had
gone, then looked up to see a great gray bird towering over
him! He leaped into the water crying, "Help, wait for
me!" But the others started laughing!

"It's a trick! Heron won't eat you. We just
wanted you to come swimming. And you've
taken to it like a duck to water!"

Maud and the Monster

Maud thought she was very brave. All the things that frightened other children were her favorites—slimy eggs, spider's legs, and even the dark.

One day, as Maud walked past the basement door, she noticed that the light was on. Without a second thought, she dashed down the stairs. But, as Maud reached the bottom step, she heard the basement door bang shut—which turned the light off!

"I'm not scared!" said Maud, defiantly. Then she noticed a strange humming sound. She crept forward, feeling along the wall, and peered slowly into the darkness. Around the corner was a bright, white monstrous shape! Maud screamed!

The basement door burst open and the light came on. Maud's mom came rushing down.

"Help, Mom! There's a monster!" cried Maud—but then, as they both looked at where she was pointing, Maud realized it was the refrigerator!

Maud felt a little silly. After that she didn't boast about her bravery anymore—well, not much!

Windy's Blowy Day

Windy the fairy was fast asleep on an orange flower.

Because Windy was fast asleep there was no wind. The leaves hung still on the trees. Tom and Ann's dad's laundry did not dry. He looked out of the window and sighed.

"We need some wind, kids," he said. "Or your school clothes won't be dry by tomorrow morning."

Tom and Ann went to the back of the yard to play with their new kite. Tom held the strings and Ann lifted the kite up, but when she let go the kite just fell to the ground.

"The kite won't fly," said Tom.

"It won't fly because there's no wind," sighed Ann.

Their voices woke Windy up. She saw the kite.

"That looks fun," she said to herself. Windy wanted to play with the kite.

Windy blew. Suddenly the kite lifted out of Ann's hands. Windy blew some more. The kite flew into the air.

"The kite's flying!" cried Tom. The kite flew high into the sky. Windy flew after it! She flitted around the kite laughing merrily.

And the laundry blew dry on the line ready for school on Monday!

Christmas Tree Fairy

It was Christmas Eve and Carly and Jordan were too excited to sleep.

"Are you still awake?" whispered Carly.

"Yes," whispered Jordan.

"Mom and Dad are asleep," whispered Carly. "Let's go downstairs and see if we can surprise Father Christmas!"

Carly and Jordan crept downstairs and peeped through the door of the living room. Everything was dark except the Christmas tree, whose lights were still twinkling.

Carly gasped. "Look!" she said. The fairy on top of the Christmas tree had come to life. She was waving her wand over the presents under the tree. Every time she waved the wand, a new present appeared.

Carly and Jordan watched until the fairy had finished her work and settled back on top of the Christmas tree, then they crept back upstairs.

The next day when they opened the presents under the tree, Mom looked a bit puzzled.

"The label says they're from me, but I don't remember buying those," she said, looking at two scarves Carly and Jordan had just opened.

"It must be magic," said Carly, smiling.

"Christmas magic," added Jordan, looking at the fairy on top of the tree.

The Magical Locket

It was Princess Crystal's birthday.
Her father, the king, had given
Princess Crystal a very special
present—a beautiful locket.

"This is a magical locket," the
king told Princess Crystal. "But,
it will only work if you say the
magic rhyme:

Magical locket, please listen well,
Help my friend with a kindly spell."

No one knew that, far away in
her tower, the wicked witch was watching Princess Crystal's
birthday in her crystal ball. When she saw the locket, the
witch wanted it for herself.

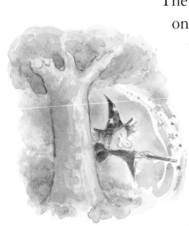

The next day, Princess Crystal went riding
on her favorite horse. She didn't see the
witch hiding behind a tree. As Princess
Crystal trotted by, the wicked witch
cast her evil spell:

"Frogs and toads, and all things black,
Throw the princess on her back!"

Princess Crystal's horse reared up
and threw her to the ground.

As quick as a flash, the wicked witch
took the locket from around Princess

Crystal's neck and threw a net over her.

"Now the locket's mine!" she cackled. She bundled the frightened princess over her shoulder and carried her away.

Soon they arrived at the witch's tower. A fierce dragon guarded it.

"Don't try to escape, my pretty one," said the witch, "or Horace the dragon will eat you up!"

At the top of the tower, the witch freed Princess Crystal.

"Recognize this?" she asked, holding up the magical locket.

"My locket!" gasped Princess Crystal.

"Yes," hissed the witch. "It's mine now. But I need the magic rhyme to go with it."

"I won't give it to you," said Princess Crystal bravely.

"Then you can stay here until you do!" shouted the witch. "Here's your precious locket," she added, throwing it at Princess Crystal. "It won't do you any good locked in here!"

She stormed out of the room, locking the door behind her.

Princess Crystal felt so alone. She leaned out of the window and began to cry. Her tears fell on Horace the dragon below.

"You're making me all wet," he said grumpily, flying up to the window. "I'm not crying, even though my wing's broken, and really hurts."

"Oh, you poor thing," said Princess Crystal, feeling sorry for the dragon. "Maybe I can help you." She closed her eyes, held the locket, and said the magic rhyme:

"Magical locket, please listen well,
Help my friend with a kindly spell."

Princess Crystal opened her eyes, and saw that Horace's wing had completely healed.

"Oh, thank you," he said happily. "My wing is healed, and I don't feel grumpy anymore. But what can I do to return your kindness?"

"Fly and find Prince Robert as quickly as you can," she said. Horace promised he'd go quickly, and beating his wings he

rose into the air. Soon, Horace found Prince Robert. When he heard that Princess Crystal had been captured by the witch, he jumped onto Horace's back and flew to the rescue.

"Thank goodness Horace found you," cried Princess Crystal, as Prince Robert climbed in through the window. But before they could escape, the door suddenly opened.

There stood the wicked witch.

"How nice of you to join us, young man," cackled the witch. "And how handsome you are! "But I think you'd look much better…as a *frog*!"

She began to cast an evil spell.

"Oh, no," thought Princess Crystal. "I'd better do something quickly."

She closed her eyes, held the locket, and whispered the magic rhyme:

"Magical locket, please listen well,
Help my friend with a kindly spell."

When Princess Crystal opened her eyes, the locket's magic had worked.

The witch's spell had backfired, and turned her into a frog instead!

"Frog spawn and slime!" croaked the frog, then hopped out of the window and was never seen again.

And Princess Crystal, Prince Robert, and Horace the dragon lived happily ever after.

Sophie's Baby

Sophie was feeling left out.

Sam was feeding his baby hamsters.

Mom was feeding baby Jake.

"What can I do?" thought Sophie.

Just then, the doorbell rang. Sophie opened the door.

"Hello, Sophie!" said the lady at the door. It was the vet. She was visiting Miss Tring next door.

"Peep has had some kittens," said the vet. "Come and see."

In Miss Tring's house there were four kittens in a box. Three kittens were gray like Peep. One was small and white.

"What's the white kitten's name?" asked Sophie.

"His name is Snowy," said Miss Tring.

Snowy was sitting in a corner of the box. The vet looked at each kitten carefully.

The three gray kittens were sucking milk from Peep's belly, but Snowy was sitting in a corner of the box on his own. He wasn't sucking milk from Peep's belly.

"Snowy needs help to feed," said the vet. She opened her bag and took out a special bottle.

Then she mixed up some warm milk in the bottle.

"Can I help feed Snowy?" asked Sophie.

"Of course," said the vet. "I'll show you what to do."

The vet put a towel on Sophie's lap and put the white kitten on it and put the bottle in Snowy's mouth.

He began to suck! Very gently, Sophie stroked Snowy with a single finger. He was so small that she didn't need to use any more.

Snowy closed his eyes.

He began to purr.

"Now I have a baby to feed," said Sophie.

Ring-a-Ring o' Roses

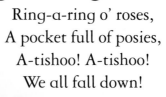

Ring-a-ring o' roses,
A pocket full of posies,
A-tishoo! A-tishoo!
We all fall down!

See a Pin and Pick It Up

See a pin and pick it up,
All the day you'll have good luck;
See a pin and let it lay,
Bad luck you'll have all the day!

Miss Mary Mack

Miss Mary Mack, Mack, Mack,
All dressed in black, black, black,
With silver buttons, buttons, buttons,
All down her back, back, back.
She went upstairs to make her bed,
She made a mistake and bumped her head;
She went downstairs to wash the dishes,
She made a mistake and washed her wishes;
She went outside to hang her clothes,
She made a mistake and hung her nose.

Mr. Nobody

Mr. Nobody is a nice young man,
He comes to the door with his hat in his hand.
Down she comes, all dressed in silk,
A rose in her bosom, as white as milk.
She takes off her gloves, she shows me her ring,
Tomorrow, tomorrow, the wedding begins.

Little Sally Waters

Little Sally Waters,
Sitting in the sun,
Crying and weeping,
For a young man.
Rise, Sally, rise,
Dry your weeping eyes,
Fly to the east,
Fly to the west,
Fly to the one you love the best.

Georgie Porgie

Georgie Porgie, pudding, and pie,
Kissed the girls and made them cry;
When the boys came out to play
Georgie Porgie ran away.

Minnie and Winnie

Minnie and Winnie
Slept in a shell.
Sleep, little ladies!
And they slept well.

Pink was the shell within,
Silver without;
Sounds of the great sea
Wandered about.

Sleep, little ladies,
Wake not soon!
Echo on echo
Dies to the moon.

Two bright stars
Peeped into the shell.
"What are they dreaming of?
Who can tell?"

Started a green linnet
Out of the croft;
Wake, little ladies,
The sun is aloft!

Lady Moon

Lady Moon, Lady Moon,
Where are you roving?
Over the sea.
Lady Moon, Lady Moon,
Whom are you loving?
All that love me.
Are you not tired with
Rolling, and never
Resting to sleep?
Why look so pale,
And so sad, as for ever
Wishing to weep?

The Case of the Crop Circles

Molly's dad was reading the newspaper. "Look at this!" he said, showing Molly a photo of some huge circles of flattened corn in Farmer Gilbert's cornfield.

"How did they get there?" asked Molly.

"No one knows, but some people say they were made by aliens," her dad replied, with a grin. "Perhaps a UFO landed on the cornfield one night!"

Molly couldn't stop thinking about the crop circles. She didn't believe they were made by aliens. It was a mystery, and she wanted to solve it.

By lunchtime, she had come up with a plan. "Carlos and I

have to do a bat watch project," she told her dad. "Would you come out with us one night to count bats? I thought we could go to Farmer Gilbert's cornfield."

Her dad smiled. "OK," he agreed. "As there's no school tomorrow, we'll go tonight."

They took a flask of hot cocoa with them up to the cornfield. The moon was shining brightly.

After a couple of hours of counting bats Molly began to feel tired. Her dad gave a loud snore beside her. Molly's own eyes began to close—and then she opened them wide again as she saw something move in the corn. She had almost missed it! Two teenage boys were creeping into the field.

Molly nudged her dad and Carlos. "Look!" she said. The boys started beating down the corn with their skateboards. They moved quickly to make a big circle.

Molly, Carlos, and her dad walked over to them. "You can stop that right now!" her dad said.

The boys looked embarrassed. "We were only having a little fun," the boys replied. "We like reading about our crop circles in the newspaper."

"If you promise you won't do this again, we won't tell on you," Molly said.

"It's a deal," the boys said, looking relieved.

Next week, Molly ran to the local store to buy the newspaper as soon as it came out.

"Look, Dad!" Molly showed him the latest photo of Farmer Gilbert's field. "No more crop circles. It says the aliens have left!"

Her dad smiled. "But we know better, don't we?" he said.

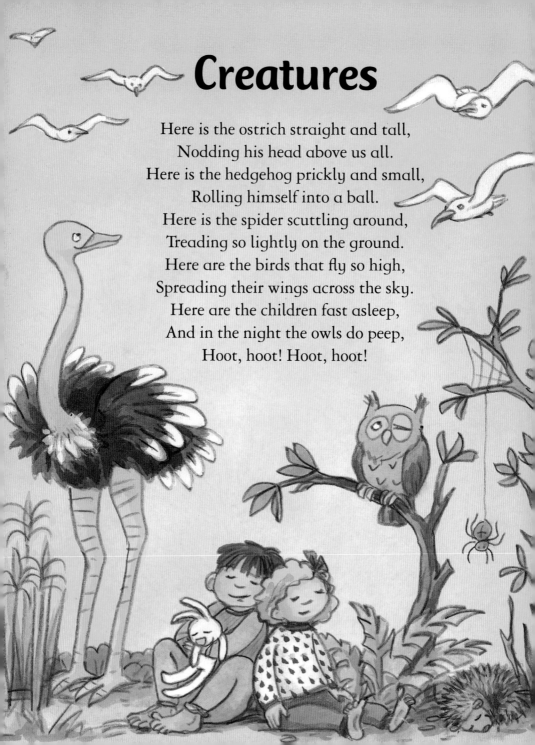

Creatures

Here is the ostrich straight and tall,
Nodding his head above us all.
Here is the hedgehog prickly and small,
Rolling himself into a ball.
Here is the spider scuttling around,
Treading so lightly on the ground.
Here are the birds that fly so high,
Spreading their wings across the sky.
Here are the children fast asleep,
And in the night the owls do peep,
Hoot, hoot! Hoot, hoot!

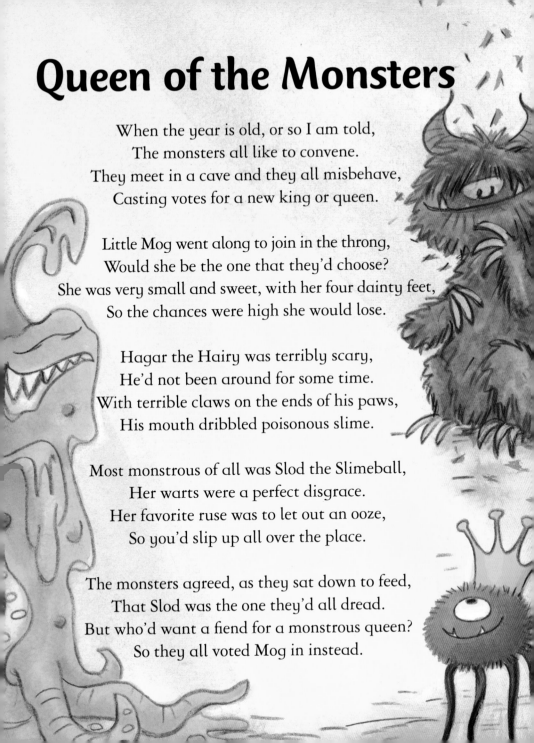

Queen of the Monsters

When the year is old, or so I am told,
The monsters all like to convene.
They meet in a cave and they all misbehave,
Casting votes for a new king or queen.

Little Mog went along to join in the throng,
Would she be the one that they'd choose?
She was very small and sweet, with her four dainty feet,
So the chances were high she would lose.

Hagar the Hairy was terribly scary,
He'd not been around for some time.
With terrible claws on the ends of his paws,
His mouth dribbled poisonous slime.

Most monstrous of all was Slod the Slimeball,
Her warts were a perfect disgrace.
Her favorite ruse was to let out an ooze,
So you'd slip up all over the place.

The monsters agreed, as they sat down to feed,
That Slod was the one they'd all dread.
But who'd want a fiend for a monstrous queen?
So they all voted Mog in instead.

The Little Turtle Dove

High in the pine tree,
The little turtle dove
Made a little nursery
To please her little love.

"Coo," said the turtle dove,
"Coo," said she;
In the long, shady branches
Of the dark pine tree.

Hey, My Kitten

Hey, my kitten, my kitten,
And hey my kitten, my deary,
Such a sweet pet as this
There is not far nor neary.
Here we go up, up, up,
Here we go down, down, downy;
Here we go backward and forward,
And here we go round, round, roundy.

Dickery, Dickery, Dare

Dickery, dickery, dare,
The pig flew up in the air.
The man in brown
Soon brought him down!
Dickery, dickery, dare.

Clap Hands

Clap hands, Daddy's coming up the wagon way,
His pockets full of money, and his hands full of clay.

Pussycat Ate the Dumplings

Pussycat ate the dumplings,
Pussycat ate the dumplings,
Mamma stood by,
And cried, "Oh fie!
Why did you eat the dumplings?"

Mrs. White

Mrs. White had a fright
In the middle of the night.
She saw a ghost, eating toast,
Halfway up a lamp post.

Lucky Digger

One day, Dad met Sophie and Sam after school.

There was a brown-and-white dog sitting at the school gate.

"Can we pat him?" asked Sophie.

Dad looked at the dog. The dog wagged his tail. "He seems friendly enough," Dad said. "Pat him gently."

Sophie and Sam patted the dog. Then Sophie noticed that he was holding up one paw and limping.

"The dog has hurt his paw!" said Sophie.

"He doesn't have a collar," said Dad. "Maybe he's a stray."

"If he's a stray, who will look after his paw?" asked Sam.

"We will," said Dad. "We will take him to the vet."

The vet cleaned the dog's paw and put a bandage on it.

"Because he doesn't have a collar, he will have to go to the dog pound," she said.

Sophie and Sam and Dad took the dog to the dog pound.

"What should we call him?" said the lady at the dog pound.

"Digger," said Sam and Sophie. Digger wagged his tail.

"What will happen to him now?" asked Sophie.

"He'll live at the dog pound until a family comes along who can give him a new home," said the lady.

"I wish Digger was our dog," said Sam a few days later.

"Can we go and see if Digger is alright?" Sophie asked Mom. "There were a lot of big dogs at the dog pound. They might be bullying Digger."

The next day Mom and Dad took Sophie and Sam to the dog pound to see Digger.

"Digger is a lucky dog," said the lady. "He has a new home."

"His new family are lucky, too," said Sophie.

"Who is Digger's new family?" said Sam.

"Well...we are!" said Mom. "We've been thinking about getting a dog for a while, and Dad and I decided last night that Digger is just perfect."

"Wow!" said Sophie and Sam.

"Woof!" said Digger, wagging his tail.

The lady smiled. "I think Digger likes you," she said.

"Are you ready to come home with us, Digger?" asked Dad.

Sam and Sophie were happy. They patted Digger.

Digger barked again. He was happy, too!

Magical Shoes

Lily the ballerina was hurrying to the theater. Today was the day of the grand ballet. Lily was dancing with her friends Wanda, Amber, and Tilly. They were all looking forward to dancing with Fleur.

Fleur was the Prima Ballerina. She always danced in a magical pair of silver ballet shoes. Only the Prima Ballerina could wear them. They would not work if anyone else wore them.

The four friends watched Fleur during the first dance as she performed a perfect plié, a beautiful arabesque, and a stunning pirouette. They all loved dancing with Fleur.

After the first dance, everyone hurried to change their costumes for the next dance. Suddenly, Fleur appeared in her bare feet, looking upset.

"Something terrible has happened!" Fleur exclaimed. "I took off my silver ballet shoes for a moment and now they have gone. I won't be able to dance until they are found."

"Don't worry," said Lily kindly. "We'll find them for you."

"We'll find the shoes in time for the next dance," Wanda promised.

The four friends ran outside. As Lily wondered which way she should go, she saw a bluejay flying toward the woods. She could see something silver in its beak.

"The silver shoes!" gasped Lily. "The bluejay must have stolen them!"

Lily ran after the bluejay as fast as she could. But meanwhile, the ballet shoes grew too heavy for the bluejay. They fell from its beak.

The shoes dropped right in front of Wanda, who was searching the woods.

"The magical shoes!" she said. "How beautiful they are. I'll just try them on quickly."

But as soon as Wanda put on the magical shoes a strange thing happened. She suddenly danced a plié. She pliéd up and down and up and down, until she realized she couldn't stop.

Wanda pliéd out of the woods and into the meadow. Soon her legs were so tired she couldn't dance anymore. She fell

flat on her back into a nearby bush.

"Are you all right?" asked Amber, who had been searching the meadow.

"Yes thanks," puffed Wanda. "But help me take the shoes off."

Amber pulled off the magical ballet shoes and gazed at them. "They're so beautiful," she said. "I'm sure no one would mind if I tried them on quickly."

Amber tried on the magical shoes and danced a perfect arabesque. "I never knew I could arabesque so well!" she thought. Then she did another, and another, until she realized that she couldn't stop.

"Help! I can't stop!" poor Amber called, as she danced out of the meadow and into the yard. She was so dizzy from dancing that she ended up in the fountain with a big splash.

Luckily, Tilly was nearby and ran to help. But when she saw the silver shoes lying on the ground, she just couldn't resist putting them on.

"They're so beautiful," she said. "I'm sure no one would mind if I tried them on quickly."

But when Tilly tried on the magical shoes, a strange thing happened. She started to pirouette around and around...

"Wheee...this is fun!" exclaimed Tilly. "I never knew I could pirouette so well!"

But then she began to spin faster and faster, and realized that she couldn't stop.

Poor Tilly pirouetted down the hill straight into a muddy puddle.

The others caught up with her and helped her up.

Lily carefully took the precious ballet shoes off Tilly's feet.

"They are so beautiful," said Lily, and she wanted to try them on, too. But in her heart, she knew that there was only one person who was meant to wear them.

"Let's return the shoes to the Prima Ballerina," Lily said to the others. "She'll be so happy we found them."

"My shoes!" exclaimed Fleur when Lily and the others returned. "Thank you! Now we must get on with the show!"

But Wanda, Amber, and Tilly were in such a mess they couldn't go back on stage.

"Oh, dear!" Fleur sighed. "You won't be able to dance looking like that." Then Fleur turned to Lily with a smile. "We will have to dance together."

Lily danced alone with the Prima Ballerina. And they danced so beautifully together that everyone clapped and cheered more than ever.

"I'll remember this evening for ever and ever," thought Lily, as she walked to the front of the stage and took her final bow.

Dizzy Ballerina Izzy

Izzy loves to ballet dance, like a lot of little girls.
She practices every day. She spins and jumps and twirls!
Izzy likes the music, and the pretty costumes, too.
But twirling is her favorite thing. It's what she loves to do.

But though she twirls so beautifully, she has a problem, too,
"I can't tell my left foot from my right! Whatever can I do?"
When all the pretty ballerinas start dancing to the right,
Izzy dances to the left. It happens every night!

"Watch where you are going!" cried Ballerina Di.
"You keep treading on my toes, when you go whirling by!"
Ballerina Zoe said, "She really has to go.
Unless she learns left and right, she's going to ruin the show!"

Dizzy Ballerina Izzy

"I give up!" poor Izzy sobbed, and ran off then to hide.
"I wish I knew my left and right. What can I do?" she cried.
"Don't be upset," said kindly Di. "I know what to do,
To help you solve the problem. Just give me your right shoe."

She tied a bell onto the toe, and sewed it with a stitch.
"When you hear it tinkle, you'll know which foot is which!"
"How wonderful!" cried Izzy, twirling to the right.
"Now I know which one is which, I'd love to dance tonight!"

So Izzy wore her special shoe. Her twirling stole the show!
"Now I can twirl up on the stage and know which way to go!"

Cats and Dogs

Hoddley, poddley, puddle and fogs,
Cats are to marry the poodle dogs;
Cats in blue jackets and dogs in red hats,
What will become of the mice and the rats?

I Bought an Old Man

Hey diddle diddle,
And hey diddle dan!
And with a little money,
I bought an old man.
His legs were all crooked
And wrong ways set on,
So what do you think
Of my little old man?

Hearts

Hearts, like doors, will open with ease
To very, very, little keys,
And don't forget that two of these
Are, "I thank you" and "If you please."

New Hay

Willy boy, Willy boy,
Where are you going?
I will go with you,
If that I may.
I'm going to the meadow
To see them a-mowing,
I am going to help them
Turn the new hay.

Two Little Dogs

Two little dogs
Sat by the fire
Over a fender of coal dust;
Said one little dog
To the other little dog,
If you don't talk, why, I must.

Mother Shuttle

Old Mother Shuttle
Lived in a coal-scuttle
Along with her dog and her cat;
What they ate I can't tell,
But 'tis known very well
That not one of the party was fat.

The Key of the Kingdom

This is the key of the kingdom:
In that kingdom is a city,
In that city is a town,
In that town there is a street,
In that street there winds a lane,
In that lane there is a yard,
In that yard there is a house,
In that house there waits a room,
In that room there is a bed,
On that bed there is a basket,
A basket of flowers.

Flowers in the basket,
Basket on the bed,
Bed in the chamber,
Chamber in the house,
House in the weedy yard,
Yard in the winding lane,
Lane in the broad street,
Street in the high town,
Town in the city,
City in the kingdom:
This is the key of the kingdom.
Of the kingdom this is the key.

Ten Green Bottles

Ten green bottles, standing on a wall,
Ten green bottles, standing on a wall,
And if one green bottle should accidentally fall,
There'd be nine green bottles, standing on a wall.

Nine green bottles, standing on a wall,
Nine green bottles, standing on a wall,
And if one green bottle should accidentally fall,
There'd be eight green bottles, standing on a wall.

Eight green bottles, standing on a wall,
Eight green bottles, standing on a wall,
And if one green bottle should accidentally fall,
There'd be seven green bottles, standing on a wall.

Seven green bottles, standing on a wall,
Seven green bottles, standing on a wall,
And if one green bottle should accidentally fall,
There'd be six green bottles, standing on a wall.

(continue with six green bottles, etc.)

As I Was Going to St. Ives

As I was going to St. Ives,
I met a man with seven wives.
Each wife had seven sacks,
Each sack had seven cats,
Each cat had seven kits.
Kits, cats, sacks, and wives,
How many were going to St. Ives?

I Saw Three Ships

I saw three ships come sailing by,
Come sailing by, come sailing by;
I saw three ships come sailing by,
On New Year's Day in the morning.

And what do you think was in them then,
Was in them then, was in them then?
And what do you think was in them then,
On New Year's Day in the morning?

Three pretty girls were in them then,
Were in them then, were in them then;
Three pretty girls were in them then,
On New Year's Day in the morning.

And one could whistle, and one could sing,
And one could play on the violin—
Such joy there was at my wedding,
On New Year's Day in the morning.

The Case of the Carnival Crasher

Molly was going to be a majorette in the town carnival. But there was bad news. "I'm sorry," said Mrs. Ellis, the majorette coach. "Our batons have disappeared. We can't practice today."

That evening, Molly's dad came home early from his brass band rehearsal. "Someone has stolen some instruments!" he said. "If we don't get them back, there won't be any music for the parade. The carnival will have to be canceled."

The next day, Molly went to see Mrs. Ellis. "Have you found our batons yet?" she asked.

"I'm afraid not, Molly," Mrs. Ellis replied.

As Molly turned to leave, she saw a trophy sitting on a shelf. It was last year's Carnival Queen trophy, and it belonged to Mrs. Ellis's daughter, Susie. Molly picked it up.

"Don't touch that!" said Susie, walking into the room.

"Susie is very proud of her trophy," said Mrs. Ellis. "But she's got to give it away soon. The new Carnival Queen will want it."

"If the carnival happens,

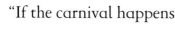

that is," muttered Susie under her breath.

Molly overheard what Susie said. "I wonder...?" she thought to herself. "Perhaps this is why everything's been disappearing!"

"Er...may I use your bathroom please, Mrs. Ellis?" asked Molly. She ran

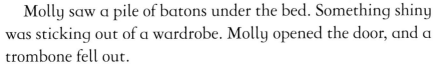

upstairs and crept into Susie's bedroom.

Molly saw a pile of batons under the bed. Something shiny was sticking out of a wardrobe. Molly opened the door, and a trombone fell out.

Molly went downstairs holding the trombone and a baton. "Are these yours, Susie?" she asked.

Susie burst into tears. "I wanted to be the Carnival Queen forever," she cried. "That's why I wanted to stop this year's carnival. I'll make it up to everyone, I promise!"

"You certainly will, Susie!" said her mom angrily.

Susie sniffed loudly. "I know," she said. "I could do face painting for all the children in the parade."

"Well, that's a start," said her mom.

Susie's face painting was a huge success. Just before the parade started, Susie presented her trophy to Lauren, the new Carnival Queen. "Congratulations!" she said. "It's good being a queen, but it's even more fun being a make up artist!"

Black Beauty Grows Up

The first place I can remember was a large meadow at Birtwick, where I lived with my mother. She always said to me, "I hope you will grow up to be gentle and good."

When I was four years old, my master broke me in. He was a good, kind man. He taught me to wear a saddle and bridle, and to carry a rider on my back. Then I learned to wear a harness, and to pull a carriage. I had iron shoes fitted to my feet. They did not hurt, but they made my feet feel very heavy.

One day in May, a man came from Squire Gordon's to take me to his home, Birtwick Park. I was put into a pleasant, airy box stall, next to a fat little gray pony, who said his name was Merrylegs. Beyond him was a tall chestnut mare called Ginger.

She looked angry. There was a stable boy called James, and the coachman who looked after us was called John Manly. He and the Squire were very pleased with me.

Mrs. Gordon decided to call me Black Beauty. On Sundays we were turned out in the paddock, and Ginger told me how cruelly she had been treated in her early life. "I never had anyone, horse or man, who was kind to me," she said. It had made her restless and bad tempered but, as the weeks passed, John Manly's patient and gentle handling made her happier.

One day in the orchard, I asked an old brown hunter called Sir Oliver how he had lost his tail. "It was cut off," he said, "right through the bone, and now I cannot brush the flies away."

"Why did they do it?" asked Ginger.

"For fashion!" said the old horse, with a stamp of his foot. "Fashion is one of the wickedest things in the world."

Soon after this, my master and mistress decided to visit friends who lived forty-six miles away. We stopped overnight at a hotel. Ginger and I were well looked after, but I woke up in the night feeling

very uncomfortable.
The stable was full
of smoke. I heard a
soft, rushing noise,
and there was a
low crackling and
snapping sound. It
made me tremble
all over.

A stable boy burst
in with a lantern and
tried to lead the horses out,
but we were all too terrified to
move. Then I heard James's voice, quiet and cheery. "Come on,
Beauty, we'll soon get you out of this."

He wrapped his scarf around my eyes, and patting and
coaxing led me out of the stable. Then he darted back for
Ginger. I gave a shrill whinny, and Ginger told me later it had
given her the courage to follow me outside. We were led away
from the burning building and spent the rest of the night in the
stables at another hotel.

When we returned home,
we heard that James
was going to a new job.
His replacement was
going to be a young boy
called Joe Green.

A few days later, John woke me in the middle of the night, and rode me at top speed to the town to fetch the doctor, because our mistress was seriously ill. I galloped as fast as I could, and became very hot, but the doctor had to ride me back again, because his own horse was exhausted.

When we got home my legs shook. I was wet through with sweat, and could only stand and pant. Joe gave me a bucketful of cold water, and some food, and left me. Soon I turned deadly cold, and ached all over.

After a long while I heard John's footsteps outside the stable. He had walked home from the doctor's. I moaned with pain.

John was horrified. He covered me with a soft blanket and gave me warm gruel to drink.

I was ill for many days, and John was very angry with Joe. When he was told Joe had only treated me that way out of ignorance, John exclaimed, "Ignorance is the worst thing in the world next to wickedness."

I often thought of these words when I came to know more of the world.

Little Husband

I had a little husband,
No bigger than my thumb;
I put him in a pint pot
And there I bade him drum.
I gave him some garters
To garter up his hose,
And a little silk handkerchief
To wipe his pretty nose.

The Robins

A robin and a robin's son
Once went to town to buy a bun.
They couldn't decide on a plum or plain,
And so they went back home again.

The Merchants of London

Hey diddle dinkety, poppety, pet,
The merchants of London they wear scarlet;
Silk in the collar and gold in the hem,
So merrily march the merchant men.

The Dame of Dundee

There was an old woman,
Who lived in Dundee,
And in her back garden
There was a plum tree;
The plums they grew rotten
Before they grew ripe,
And she sold them
Three farthings a pint.

Christmas Eve

On Christmas Eve I turned the spit,
I burned my fingers, I feel it yet;
The little cock sparrow flew over the table,
The pot began to play with the ladle.

Gingerbread Men

Smiling girls, rosy boys,
Come and buy my little toys:
Monkeys made of gingerbread,
And sugar horses painted red.

Egg Raiders

Zac and Lili lived in a nature reserve on Karlin Island. They loved living there. They had a lot of fun and some wonderful adventures.

"Do you want to come with me to see the gannets?" Mom asked Zac and Lili one day.

"Yes, please!" they said together.

Gannets were rare seabirds that lived on Black Rock, a small craggy island nearby.

"I hope some of the eggs have hatched," said Lili, as they sailed over to Black Rock. "I can't wait to see the chicks!"

As soon as they had landed, Zac and Lili ran off to the other side of the island.

Suddenly, Zac grabbed Lili's arm. "Look at those men!" he said, pointing.

Lili looked. "Oh no! They're stealing the gannet eggs!" she gasped.

"We can't let them get away," said Zac. "We have to do something."

Zac started running toward the beach. "If we let their boat go they can't escape. Come on, Lili!" he called.

Lili followed him. They both ran as fast as they could.

They found the thieves' boat, moored on the beach.

It was difficult to untie the knot but at last they managed it. Lili and Zac watched the boat float away, and then went to tell Mom what was happening.

"Good work," she said, when she heard what they had done. Then she phoned the coast guard and told him about the thieves.

"I'll be right there," he said. "Leave those thieves to me."

The thieves were looking for their boat when the coast guard arrived.

"You two had better come with me," he said sternly, taking the eggs from them.

When the gannets saw the men being taken away, they started making loud calls.

"I think they're pleased the men are gone!" said Lili.

"Or maybe they're saying thank you—to you!" said Mom.

Mary Had a Little Lamb

Mary had a little lamb,
Its fleece was white as snow,
And everywhere that Mary went
The lamb was sure to go.

It followed her to school one day,
Which was against the rule;
It made the children laugh and play
To see a lamb in school.

Song of the Stars

We are the stars that sing,
We sing with our light.
We are the birds of fire
We fly over the sky,
Our light is a voice.
We make a road for spirits,
For the spirits to pass over.
Among us are three hunters
Who chase a bear;
There never was a time
When they were not hunting.
We look down on the mountains.
This is the song of the stars.

In the Treetop

Rock-a-bye, baby, up in the treetop!
Mother his blanket is spinning;
And a light little rustle that never will stop,
Breezes and boughs are beginning.
Rock-a-bye, baby, swinging so high!
Rock-a-bye!

When the wind blows, then the cradle will rock.
Hush! now it stirs in the bushes;
Now with a whisper, a flutter of talk,
Baby and hammock it pushes.
Rock-a-bye, baby! Shut, pretty eye!
Rock-a-bye!

Mother Hubbard

Old Mother Hubbard went to the cupboard
To get her poor doggy a bone;
But when she got there the cupboard was bare,
And so the poor doggy had none.

She went to the tailor's
To buy him a coat
But when she got back
He was riding a goat.

She went to the cobbler's
To buy him some shoes,
But when she got back
He was reading the news.

She went to the hosier's
To buy him some hose
When she got back
He was dressed in his clothes.

The dame made a curtsey,
The dog made a bow,
The dame said, "Your servant,"
The dog said, "Bow wow."

Shy Ballerina Di

Ballerina Di was as dainty as can be.
No other ballerina danced as daintily as she.
When she skipped with other girls, holding hands together,
They said she danced as lightly as a cloud or floating feather!

One day, the teacher told the class, "There's going to be a show.
I want to give the leading role to dainty Di, you know."
"I'm far too shy!" protested Di, "I'd really rather not,
Already, I feel nervous—my stomach's in a knot!"

No matter what the others said, Di firmly shook her head.
"I think the teacher should choose someone else instead!"
So Zoe got the leading part, to nervous Di's relief
(Though Di did feel a little disappointed underneath).

Shy Ballerina Di

Everybody practiced hard, to learn their ballet parts.
Until all the dancers knew at last every step by heart!
Finally, the first night came, but then disaster struck.
Zoe fell and hurt her foot. It really was bad luck!

"You can't dance the leading part. Whatever should we do?
Shy Di is the only one who knows the part like you!"
Shy Di looked at all her friends. "I'll dance the part," she sighed.
"I can't let my friends down. At least I will have tried!"

She trembled as the curtain rose, but as the music played,
Di could not believe it! "I just don't feel afraid!"
Di danced as she had never danced. The crowd all called for more.
"What a dainty dancer! She's a star, for sure!"

315

Little Kitten

Snuggle up, kitten, warm in your bed.
Let moonlit dreams fill your head.

The little bunny curled up tight,
Dreams of carrots every night.

The baby mouse dreams in his nest,
Of cheese, the food that he loves best.

Shut your eyes, kitten, sleep and dream,
Of balls of yarn, and bowls of cream.

Mr. Moon will guard your bed.
Good night, sleep tight, sleepyhead!

Cuddly Kittens

Five little pussy cats, playing near the door,
One ran and hid inside and then there were four.

Four little pussy cats, underneath a tree,
One heard a doggie bark and then there were three.

Three little pussy cats, thinking what to do,
One saw a tiny bird and then there were two.

Two little pussy cats, sitting in the sun,
One tried to catch his tail and then there was one.

One little pussy cat, looking for some fun,
Saw a pretty butterfly and then there was none.

Five little pussy cats, snuggled in a heap,
They've had a very busy day, but now they're fast asleep!

Smoky the Dragon

Smoky the dragon lived next door to Emma. Every day, Emma went to elementary school and Smoky went to dragon school. And every day after school, Emma and Smoky played together. The best game was when Smoky breathed smoke from his nose. He could do a lot of clever smoke tricks.

But one day after school, Smoky didn't want to play. He started to cry. "I don't like school," he sniffed. "All the other dragons are clever. They can light fires and boil water and even make toast! I can only breathe smoke from my nose."

Emma hugged Smoky, but she didn't know what to say.

The next day it was Emma's birthday party. Marvo the magician was coming to do some magic tricks.

Halfway through the birthday lunch the phone rang.

"Oh dear," said Mom when she got off the phone. "Marvo's ill. He won't be able to come. I don't know what to do."

"We can do clever tricks," said three of the dragons. "We can boil water and light fires and make toast!"

"They aren't party tricks," said Mom.

"Smoky can do a lot of clever smoke tricks," said Emma.

So Smoky made smoke curl and swirl and made smoke rings to jump through.

"What a clever dragon!" said Mom.

And Smoky smiled a big smoky smile!

A Tiger for Tara

It was Saturday morning. Tara was very excited. She was going to the pet store to buy a pet.

"What pet shall we buy?" asked Mom, on the way to the pet store.

"Let's buy a hippo," said Tara.

"Oh, no," said Mom. "A hippo is too fat."

"Let's buy an elephant," said Tara.

"Oh, no," said Mom. "An elephant is too big."

"Let's buy a snake," said Tara.

"Oh, no," said Mom. "A snake is too long and wiggly."

Outside the pet store was a boy with a toy tiger. "I definitely want to buy a tiger," said Tara. "A tiger would be the best pet."

Inside the pet store there were big pets and small pets, fat pets and thin pets. But there were no tigers at all.

"These pets are good," said Tara. "But a tiger would be better."

"We can't have a tiger," said Mom. "They are too fierce."

"Wait here," said the pet store owner. He went into the back room and came back out with a basket of kittens. There were black-and-white kittens and one small stripy kitten.

"This kitten's name is Tiger," said the owner. "Would you like him as a pet?"

"Oh yes!" said Tara. She gave Tiger a hug. "Tiger is the best pet of all."

Man Overboard!

Zac and Lili had been to the
mainland with Dad to
fetch supplies. They
boarded the ferry to
sail home to
Karlin Island.

Dad found a friend to
talk with, so Zac and Lili
went off to look around.

"Be careful," Dad shouted after them.

"We will," they promised. Zac and Lili headed up to the
deck so they could look out for dolphins.

"Look at that little boy, Zac," Lili gasped, pointing. "That's
so dangerous."

A young boy was sitting on the top of the ferry rail.

Suddenly, the ferry hit a large wave and tipped to the side.
The boy slipped and fell into the sea.

Lili and Zac rushed over to the rail.

"Help!" the boy shouted, waving his arms. "I can't swim!"

"I'll throw him the life preserver," Zac told Lili. "You go and
tell the captain to stop the ferry."

Lili ran off toward the captain's cabin shouting for help. Zac
lifted the life preserver off its hook and tossed it to the boy. The
boy stretched out his arms and grabbed it.

"Hold tight!" Zac called. "Lili's gone to get help. You'll soon be out of there." Zac knew it was important for the boy to keep calm.

The ferry stopped moving. Zac smiled. Fast work, Lili!

The captain came hurrying over, with Lili, Dad, and the boy's worried parents.

"I'll lower the lifeboat," the captain said.

Dad offered to row the lifeboat.

"Careful, Dad!" cried Lili anxiously. "The waves are big!"

Dad rowed carefully out to the boy and pulled him into the lifeboat.

Before long the boy was back onboard, wrapped in a blanket.

"Thank you for saving me," the boy said to Lili and Zac. "I'll never sit on the rail again!"

The Wedding

Pussycat, wussicat, with a white foot,
When is your wedding and I'll come to it.
The beer's to brew, and the bread's to bake,
Pussycat, wussicat, don't be too late.

First

First in a carriage,
Second in a gig,
Third on a donkey,
And fourth on a pig.

Gee Up, Neddy

Gee up, Neddy,
Don't you stop,
Just let your feet go
Clippety clop.
Clippety clopping,
Round and round.
Giddy up,
We're homeward bound.

Slowly, Slowly

Slowly, slowly, very slowly
Creeps the garden snail.
Slowly, slowly, very slowly
Up the garden rail.

Quickly, quickly, very quickly
Runs the little mouse.
Quickly, quickly, very quickly
Round about the house.

Hark! Hark!

Hark, hark,
The dogs do bark,
Beggars are coming to town:
Some in rags,
Some in tags,
And some in velvet gowns.

The Little Bird

This little bird flaps its wings,
Flaps its wings, flaps its wings,
This little bird flaps its wings,
And flies away in the morning!

My Little Puppy

Everyone agreed that Isobel's little puppy, Patches, looked
adorable. He had stumpy legs and a round, chubby belly,
silky-soft ears, lively brown eyes, and a small patch just over
his right eye.

Isobel loved Patches and Patches loved Isobel.

The only problem was that Patches was always getting
himself—and Isobel—into trouble.

A lot of trouble!

On Monday, Patches chewed one of Dad's slippers…and the
strap on Mom's new handbag.

"Can't that animal chew on his toy?" complained Dad.

"He doesn't like it," sighed Isobel, trying to give Patches the
rubber bone she had bought for him. Patches
put his paws on Isobel's hands and licked
them.

"That tickles," giggled Isobel.
It was impossible to be angry
with Patches for long.
On Tuesday, Patches
pulled the clothes off
the laundry line and
dragged them
through the soil.
The clothes were
all dirty.

"Oh, Patches, not again!" complained Dad.
"He was only trying to play," defended
Isobel. "He's really sorry, aren't you,
Patches?"

Patches barked and
rolled over on his back,
waving his legs in the air.
Even Dad had to laugh.

On Wednesday, Patches
knocked over a vase.

"He was only trying to smell the flowers," said Isobel.
Patches put his head on one side and barked softly.
"See," said Isobel. "He's saying 'sorry,' aren't you, Patches?"
Mom grinned. "All right, but be more careful!"
Later that day Mrs. May, who lived next door, was in her
yard. Her white cat, Snowy, jumped on top of the fence and
hissed at Patches.
Patches barked back.
"Please don't let that puppy frighten poor
Snowy," called Mrs. May.
"We'll make sure Patches stays out
of Snowy's way," said Mom.
"Yes, please do," sniffed
Mrs. May. "Poor Snowy!"
"Poor Snowy, indeed,"
muttered Isobel. "That cat is
always teasing Patches."

"Now, now, Isobel," soothed Mom. "Mrs. May was telling me earlier that she's lost her gold ring. I think her husband gave it to her a long time ago. She's very upset about it, and that probably makes her seem more angry than she really is. And you know she loves Snowy as much as you love Patches."

Mom was right. Mrs. May and Snowy were best friends.

The next day Isobel and Patches were in the yard with Mom and Dad, when Mrs. May came out of her house.

"Any sign of your ring?" called Mom. Mrs. May shook her head sadly. "I think I've lost it for good," she said.

Just then, Snowy jumped down from the fence, scratched Patches across his nose with her paw, then ran off.

"Snowykins!" cried Mrs. May. "Bad cat!"

Patches squeezed through a hole in the fence and began to chase Snowy around and around Mrs. May's yard. Isobel and her parents followed. Around and around they went—till Dad caught Patches.

"Oh, no! Look at my vegetables!" cried Mrs. May. "And my poor flowers!"

"We're so sorry," said Isobel's mom. "We'll help you replant them."

"That would be very kind," said Mrs. May.

Mom and Mrs. May picked up the plant pots and the gardening tools. Dad tied together the runner-bean poles that had been knocked over. And Isobel and Patches dug holes to put back some of the flowers that had been disturbed.

"What's that, Patches?" asked Isobel, as Patches pushed a lump of soil toward her with his nose. Isobel scraped away the soil, then leaped to her feet.

"Mrs. May! Mrs. May! Patches has found your ring!"

Mrs. May was delighted. "Oh, you clever puppy!" she said, patting Patches' head. "How can I ever thank you?"

And after that, Isobel, Patches, and Mrs. May were the best of friends.

Although Patches still sometimes chased Snowy around and around the garden!

Dolphin Finds a Star

One night in the moonlight, a baby dolphin called Splash looked up and saw a shooting star. It zoomed across the sky and disappeared.

"That star has fallen into the water!" Splash cried. "I'm going to find it and give it to my mommy as a present. She loves shiny things."

In the distance Splash saw something sparkling. He swam toward the sparkles, thinking it was the star.

But when he got closer, he saw that it was a shoal of flashing fish, wiggling and weaving through the water.

Then Splash saw something glowing above his head. "There's the star! My mommy will be so pleased," he thought happily, and he swam toward the shining light.

But when he got closer, Splash found that the light was a lamp shining on the very top of a sailing boat.

The more the baby dolphin swam around, the more shiny creatures he saw. There were flashing fish, jiggly jellyfish, and even sparkly sea horses, but the fallen star was nowhere to be found.

At last, Splash saw a light that was much brighter than all the rest. He swam toward it, hoping it would be the star. He swam through an underwater garden of swirling seaweed and shimmering shells. And then, at last, he found the star. It was in the hair of a beautiful mermaid queen sitting on her throne.

"Hello, baby dolphin. What brings you here?" she asked, but Splash felt very shy. He didn't know what to say.

So the flashing fish, the jiggly jellyfish, and the sparkly sea horses all told the mermaid queen:

"He was looking for the star that's in your hair. He wanted to give it to his mommy."

"In that case, you shall have it," said the mermaid, and she handed the shining star to Splash.

Splash gave his mommy the star and she was very pleased. Together they played with it all day long.

Then, when night came, they jumped up as high as they could and pushed the star back up into the sky, where it could shine down on everyone—on the flashing fish and the jiggly jellyfish, on the sparkly sea horses and on you, too.

What a Bad Goat!

Farmer Jim was doing his rounds to see all the animals on the farm.

Pig was looking after her ten piglets.
"What a good pig!" said Jim.
Hen was laying a big brown egg.
"What a good hen!" said Jim.
Horse was eating a bale of hay.
"What a good horse!" said Jim.
Cow was being milked.
"What a good cow!" said Jim.
Duck was swimming on the pond.
"What a good duck!" said Jim.
Cat was chasing mice.
"What a good cat!" said Jim.
Dog was watching the farm gate.
"What a good dog!" said Jim.

Jim went back to the farmhouse. "I wonder where Goat is?" he said to himself. Then he saw! Goat was in the farmhouse yard eating the laundry. He had already eaten six socks, and he was starting on a dress.

Jim chased Goat away from the laundry line. "What a bad goat!" he said.

Silly Pig

One day, Pansy Pig decided to go and look for treasure.

"You silly pig!" said the other animals. "You won't find treasure on the farm."

First, Pansy saw a sparkling necklace in the tree.

"Treasure!" she said. "I will put it around my neck."

But the sparkling necklace wasn't really a necklace. It was a spiderweb sparkling with raindrops.

Spider was very angry. "You silly pig!" she said.

Pansy saw some red earrings in the hedge.

"Treasure!" she said. "I will put them on my ears."

But the red earrings weren't really earrings. They were red berries.

Blackbird's nest was next to the red berries. She was very angry. "You silly pig!" she said.

Then Pansy saw something sparkling in the mud.

"Treasure!" she said. And this time...it really was treasure!

Farmer Kate was in the farmyard.

"Hello, Pansy!" she said. "What have you got there?" She took the treasure.

"You've found my ring!" said Kate. "You clever pig!"

Beach Rescue

Zac and Lili were worried. They hadn't seen their favorite dolphin, Whistler, for a while.

"Dolphins sometimes swim very far out to sea," Mom told them. "I'm sure Whistler will be back soon."

But there was no sign of Whistler the next day. Or the next.

"What if something has happened to him?" said Lili.

"Can we go and look for him, Dad?" begged Zac.

"Okay," Dad agreed. "But I'm sure he's fine."

They all set off in Dad's boat.

After a while, they saw some dolphins ahead.

"Let's get a bit closer and see if Whistler is among them," said Dad. But although they looked carefully Whistler was nowhere to be seen.

Now Lili and Zac were really worried. Where was Whistler?

To their surprise the dolphins started to surround the boat. They whistled and leaped in the air. They swam away for a bit and then came back again.

"I think they want us to follow them, Dad!" said Zac.

"You may be right!" agreed Dad.

The dolphins led them to a nearby island. As they got closer, Lili saw another dolphin lying on the beach.

"It's Whistler!" she shouted. "He must be injured!"

Dad moored the boat and they all ran over to Whistler.

"What happened to him?" asked Zac.

"He must have swum too close to the island, then got stranded when the tide went out," Dad explained. "If we don't get him back into the sea soon, he will die," he added quietly.

"Oh no!" cried Lili and Zac.

"We must keep Whistler wet until Dolphin Rescue arrive," he said.

They got buckets from the boat and began pouring seawater over Whistler.

At last, Dolphin Rescue arrived. Carefully, they helped Whistler back into the sea.

The dolphin swam off. Then he leaped out of the water with a big splash and clicked happily.

"I think he's saying thank you!" laughed Dad.

"Bye, Whistler!" called Lili and Zac together.

Sam Duckling Swims

Sam Duckling lived by the pond with Mommy Duck and the other ducklings.

"Jump in and swim," said Mommy Duck one day. *Splash!* All the little ducklings jumped in and swam—except Sam.

"Jump in and swim," said Mommy Duck. "It's fun!"

Sam put his wing into the water.

"The water's too cold," he said. "And it looks very deep. I'll stay here."

"Quack! Quack!" quacked the other ducklings. "Swim with us, Mommy! Swim with us!"

Mommy Duck went off to swim with the other ducklings, leaving Sam all alone on the bank. He began to cry.

Just then Frog popped his head out of the water. "Hi, Sam," he said. "I'll help you swim."

Frog got a lily pad. "Sit on the lily pad, Sam," he said. Sam sat on the lily pad and Frog pulled Sam along.

"Now splash your feet," said Frog. Sam splashed his feet.

"This is fun!" quacked Sam.

"Now get off the lily pad," said Frog. Sam got off the lily pad.

"I'm swimming!" he cried.

"Well done!" quacked Mommy Duck.

Lost in the Jungle

One summer, Rachel and her mom and dad went on a jungle safari for their vacation.

Rachel packed a map and compass.

"You won't need a map and compass," said Dad. "We're going to a part of the jungle where there are special paths to follow."

Rachel still packed her map and compass.

When they arrived in the jungle, Rachel got out her map and compass. "We're here," she said, putting a big cross on the map.

"We don't need a map and compass," said Dad. "Follow me!" They climbed into their jeep and went deep into the jungle. At a junction a sign said, "To the pool."

"We're going north," said Rachel.

"Great!" said Dad.

Soon they came to the pool. Rachel looked at her map. "We're here," she said, putting another cross on the map.

They took a lot of photographs of the animals at the pool. Then Dad said, "Time we went back to camp."

They went back along the path, but when they got to the junction the sign was gone.

"Don't worry," said Rachel. "We can follow my map."

Soon they were back at the camp. "You were right, Rachel," said Dad, laughing. "We did need a map and compass."

What Do You Think?

There was an old woman, and what do you think?
She lived upon nothing but victuals and drink:
Victuals and drink were the chief of her diet;
This tiresome old woman could never be quiet.

The Baby in the Cradle

The baby in the cradle
Goes rock-a-rock-a-rock.
The clock on the dresser
Goes tick-a-tick-a-tock.

The rain on the window
Goes tap-a-tap-a-tap,
But here comes the sun,
So we clap-a-clap-a-clap!

A Cat Came Fiddling

A cat came fiddling out of a barn,
With a pair of bagpipes under her arm;
She could sing nothing but, "Fiddle cum fee,
The mouse has married the bumblebee."
Pipe, cat—dance, mouse,
We'll have a wedding at our good house.

Bobby Shaftoe

Bobby Shaftoe's gone to sea,
Silver buckles at his knee;
When he comes back
He'll marry me,
Bonny Bobby Shaftoe!

Dance to Your Daddy

Dance to your daddy,
My little babby;
Dance to your daddy,
My little lamb.

You shall have a fishy,
In a little dishy;
You shall have a fishy
When the boat comes in.

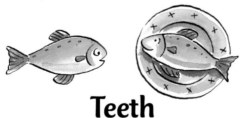

Teeth

Thirty white horses upon a red hill,
Now they tramp, now they champ,
Now they stand still.

Black Beauty's New Owners

I had been living happily at Squire Gordon's for three years when we were told that because the Squire's wife was ill, she would have to leave England to live in a warmer country. The gray pony Merrylegs was given to Mr. Blomefield, the vicar, and Joe went to look after him. Ginger and I were sold to an earl, who lived in a very large house called Earlshall Park.

John, Squire Gordon's coachman, told the new coachman, Mr. York, all about us. The following day we were harnessed to the carriage to take out the lady of the house, and our heads were held up unnaturally high with bearing reins.

When we had to go up a steep hill I could not put my head forward and pull the carriage up as usual, but took all the strain on my back and legs. I began to dread having my harness put on, and Ginger said, "I can't bear it, and I won't."

Each day our heads were reined up tighter. One day Ginger reared up and kicked right over the carriage pole, then fell down, kicking me as she did so.

We were both sore and bruised. Ginger was never put in the carriage again and I had a new partner called Max.

In the spring the family went to London. They left a groom, Reuben Smith, in charge of the horses. One day he drove me to town in the carriage to get it repaired, and was to ride me home. He left me at an inn, and got back very late. The stable boy said I had a loose shoe, but Reuben took no notice and set off at a gallop. My shoe came off, and still he galloped, over roughly laid sharp stones.

My foot split and, in terrible pain, I stumbled and fell on both knees, throwing Smith off.

After many hours, some men from the house came out to search for us. They found us and led me slowly home. In time, my knees healed, but they were badly scarred. Ginger, too, had been injured by hard riding. She was to be rested, but I was to be sold. My owner said, "I cannot have knees like that in my stables."

I went to a livery stable as a "job-horse." This meant I could be hired out to anyone who wanted to drive me. Many people had no consideration for me at all, and treated me as if I were an engine.

One day a good driver hired me, and I was sold to his friend, Mr. Barry. But his groom left the stable dirty, and I got an infection in my feet. After this, I was sent to a horse fair to be sold again.

There are all kinds of horses and ponies at a horse fair, and all kinds of buyers.

Some are very rough, but a small, gentle, cheerful man said to me, "Well, old boy, I think we should suit each other."

He bought me and rode me home, and I became a London cab horse.

My new owner, Jerry Barker, had his own cab. An old war horse called Captain did the morning work, and I did the afternoons. We worked hard, but our master treated us well and we had a day of rest every Sunday.

One bitterly cold New Year's Eve, our passengers kept us waiting for hours and, when we got home, Jerry became ill with a bad cough and a fever. He almost died and had to give up cab work, and so I was sold again.

It was then that began the most dreadful period of my life.

I Hear Thunder

I hear thunder, I hear thunder,
Hark don't you? Hark don't you?
Pitter patter raindrops, pitter patter raindrops,
I'm wet through. So are you!

I see blue skies, I see blue skies,
Way up high, way up high.
Hurry up the sunshine, hurry up the sunshine,
We'll soon dry! We'll soon dry!

Getting Dressed

We're going out to play, but first we must get dressed!
I'll start with my undershirt. It goes on my chest.
I need to find my underpants. They're my favorite—spotted red!
I wonder where they are…Oh! They're right here on my bed!

Where's my yellow T-shirt? I can't see it anywhere.
I'll look inside my closet…Yes! It's hanging there!
Next, my denim pants—I saw them just last night!
I left them on the chair, I think…Yes! They're here, I'm right.

Now if only I could find my socks, then I could put them on!
My red socks should be in the drawer…where have they gone?
Okay, now I've found my socks, then I can put on shoes,
I've got two pairs right by my bed—which ones should I choose?

I'll need my warm green sweater that's made of fluffy wool,
I've found it in my toy box—all I have to do is pull!
I've got my coat—I'm ready! But there's one thing left to do.
I'll have to dress my teddy. Oh! Looks like Teddy's ready, too!

Showy Ballerina Zoe

Ballerina Zoe could leap high off the ground,
And land so very gracefully, she'd barely make a sound!
But although she was so graceful, it went right to her head.
Instead of practicing her steps, she used to boast instead.

It made the other dancers angry. "We're fed up with Zoe.
Why does she have to brag so much, and be so proud and showy?"
One day, Zoe had some news: "I've heard about a show.
There's going to be an audition. I think we all should go!

I know that I will win a part. Of that, you can be sure.
But you might get a little role, if you would practice more."
The day of the audition came. "I'll stretch and do some bends,
To warm up ready for the test," said Zoe to her friends.

But as she stretched her tutu ripped. The others heard it tear!
"What should I do?" Zoe cried. "I've nothing else to wear."
"Don't worry!" Dizzy Izzy cried. "We'll dance around you.
Then no one else will ever see the big hole in your tutu!"

So Di and Izzy twirled about, with Zoe in between.
Zoe was delighted. "We make a splendid team!
Now each of us has won a part, it's very plain to see,
Not only are you great friends, you can dance as well as me!"

Tidal Pool Friends

Sid the seahorse was playing hide-and-seek with his friends on the coral reef.

"Three...two...one..." he counted.

Suddenly, there was a whooshing noise. *Splash!* A big wave crashed over the reef and tumbled him over and over.

When Sid stopped tumbling, he opened his eyes. Everything looked strange. "This isn't a reef," he decided. "It looks like a tidal pool."

He sat on a shiny shell to decide what to do, feeling lonely.

"Do you mind?" snapped a voice inside the shell. "You're sitting on my house." It was a little hermit crab called Katy.

"Sorry," said Sid. "I didn't think anyone lived here."

Katy clicked her claws loudly. "It's safe to come out!" she cried. All at once, orange starfish, pink shrimp, red crabs, yellow and green sea anemones, and shimmering fish appeared.

"Wow!" gasped Sid. "Your home is just as colorful as my home on the coral reef." Then he sighed a little sigh.

"What's the matter?" asked Katy.

"Do you think I'll ever see my home again?" asked Sid.

"Of course you will," smiled Katy. "You just need to catch a wave. The tide is going out. If you hurry, you'll get a ride at once."

"Bye, bye, everyone," cried Sid, as a wave carried him off.

"Bye, Sid! Come back any time," shouted Katy.

And that's exactly what Sid did!

The Flyaway Fairy

One day, some little fairies were learning to
fly. Poppy, Fern, and Rosie were very good,
but Daisy was scared of falling.

"I don't want to fly," she whispered.

Daisy's best friend was Caterpillar.
"Can you teach me to fly?" she asked him.

"I don't have any wings," said Caterpillar.
"But I'm sure someone will help."

Caterpillar took Daisy to see Bumblebee.

"Will you teach me to fly?" asked Daisy.

"Buzz buzz! Sorry! I don't have time!" Bumblebee replied.
"I'm too busy collecting nectar from the flowers."

So Caterpillar took Daisy to see his friend Bluebird.

"Can you teach me to fly?" asked Daisy.

"I'm sorry, I'm afraid I can't leave my chicks," replied Bluebird.

It seemed that no one wanted to teach Daisy to fly.

But a few days later Daisy got a big surprise. She was
sitting on a flower feeling sorry for herself when a beautiful
creature fluttered toward her and called out, "Hello, Daisy!
It's me...Caterpillar! I've changed into a butterfly.
Now that I have wings, I can teach you to fly.
It's easy!"

Daisy's friend taught her to fly in no time.

"Now I know how to do it, I don't feel
scared any more," Daisy laughed.

Stranded

Dad had to check on some seal pups near Black Rock, so Lili and Zac went with him.

"They're so cute," said Lili, smiling.

"They're all fit and healthy, too," said Dad, looking pleased.

They set off home again to Karlin Island, but they hadn't gone very far when Zac noticed water swishing around his feet. "Dad! The boat's leaking!" he shouted.

Lili looked. "The water's coming in fast, too!" she gasped. "It must be a big hole!"

Dad quickly got a bucket. "Let's try and bail the water out," he said. "I'll head back to Black Rock."

But the water was coming in too fast. Soon it was almost up to Lili's knees.

"Dad! The boat's sinking!" she cried.

"Don't panic. Look, we're almost there," said Dad, pointing to the craggy island not far ahead. "We can swim the rest of the way."

They jumped overboard in their life jackets, and swam through the ocean.

"I'll phone for help," Dad said

when they were safely on Black Rock. But his cell phone had disappeared. "Oh no! It must have fallen out of my pocket into the ocean," he groaned.

Lili and Zac were cold, wet, and miserable.

"Don't worry, Mom will come looking for us soon," Dad told them.

"But how will she know where to find us?" asked Lili.

Dad thought about that. "We'll light a fire," he decided. "When Mom sees the smoke, she'll come to find out what's going on."

They collected some dry branches and twigs, and Dad rubbed two twigs together to spark the fire to life.

They all huddled around the fire to keep warm.

Before long Lili saw a motorboat chugging toward them. It was the coast guard.

Then they heard a familiar voice coming through the coast guard's bullhorn.

It was Mom!

"Need some help over there?" she asked.

"Hooray!" cheered Zac loudly.

"We'll soon be home now," said Dad cheerfully.

Polar Bear and the Rainbow

Ben, the little polar bear, was the same color as snow. He was the same color as his sister and his mom.

He was the same color as polar bears everywhere.

"How boring," thought Ben.

Ben watched the sunrise with his friends, the hare and the fox. "You look pink in the new sunlight," they told him.

"I'm pink! I'm pink!" cried Ben. But as the sun climbed higher, he turned back to the color of snow.

Ben went swimming with his friend the seal.

"You look blue in the water," she told him.

"I'm blue! I'm blue!" cried Ben. But when he climbed out of the water, he turned back to the color of his sister and his mom.

That night, Ben dreamed that he was as bright and sparkly as a rainbow. But when he woke up his rainbow fur had gone.

The next day, Ben found a snowman. He had a big smile made of stones.

"The snowman is the same color as me, and he looks very happy," thought Ben.

Then Ben played hide-and-seek with his friends.

"The snow is the same color as me. That's why I'm good at hide-and-seek," thought Ben.

Soon sparkly white snowflakes began to fall all around. The snowflakes felt tingly on Ben's nose.

"Snowflakes are the same color as me, and they are beautiful," thought Ben.

At the end of the day, Ben cuddled up with his family.

"I don't mind being polar bear-colored after all. I am the same color as snowmen and snowflakes," he thought.

Best of all, he was the same color as his sister and his mom. They were soft and snuggly, like polar bears everywhere, and he loved them very much.

Give Me a Hug!

Missy was a very daring little mouse. She liked to swing from willow branches...until one day she fell off!

Then Missy didn't feel daring at all. She stumbled back home to her mom.

"Give me a hug!" wailed Missy.

"Of course I will," said Mom. She stroked poor Missy's aching head and, very quietly, she said, "How's that? Does that take away the pain? Here's a hug to help you feel better again." Then she hugged Missy tight.

And Missy did feel better. Missy was a very cheerful little mouse. She smiled as she helped. She hummed as she played. But one day, when Missy lost her favorite teddy, she didn't feel cheerful at all. She ran downstairs to her mom.

"Give me a hug!" wailed Missy.

"Of course I will," said Mom.

She told Missy to look under the bed, and when Missy found Teddy there, Mom gently said, "I knew you'd find Teddy. You see, I wasn't wrong. Have a hug and I don't think those tears will last long." Then she hugged Missy tight.

And Missy began to smile. Missy was a very brave little mouse. She liked to sneak up to the farm cat and tickle his whiskers.

That night, though, Missy heard noises under the bed. And she didn't feel brave at all. She crept along to her mom's room.

"Give me a hug!" wailed Missy.

"Of course I will," said Mom.

After Mom had given Missy a hug, she took Missy back to her room and looked under the bed. Then, as she tucked Missy in, Mom smiled and said, "Missy, I've looked and I promise you there's nothing there."

One morning when Mom was really very busy, Missy came running into the room.

"Give me a hug!" she pleaded.

"What's happened now?" asked Mom. Missy smiled. "Nothing! It's just...your hugs make me happy!"

"That's good," said her mom, "because I like it when you ask me if I'll hug you. Our hugs are the best thing, and I love them, too!"

A Thorn

I went to the wood and got it;
I sat me down and looked at it;
The more I looked at it the less I liked it;
And I brought it home because I couldn't help it.

Cross Patch

Cross patch,
Draw the latch,
Sit by the fire and spin;
Take a cup,
And drink it up,
Then call your neighbors in.

Baa, Baa, Black Sheep

Baa, baa, black sheep, have you any wool?
Yes, sir, yes, sir, three bags full;
One for the master, one for the dame,
And one for the little boy that lives down the lane.

Go to Bed Late

Go to bed late,
Stay very small;
Go to bed early,
Grow very tall.

Pussycat Mole

Pussycat Mole,
Jumped over a coal,
And in her best petticoat
Burned a great hole.
Poor pussy's weeping,
She'll have no more milk,
Until her best petticoat's
Mended with silk.

On the Grassy Banks

On the grassy banks
Lambkins at their pranks;
Woolly sisters, woolly brothers,
Jumping off their feet,
While their woolly mothers
Watch them and bleat.

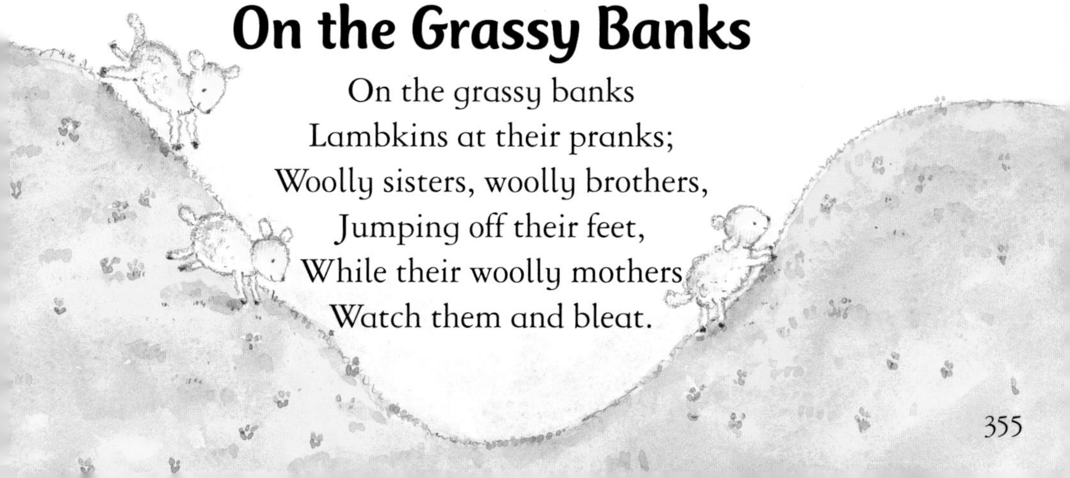

Brave Little Deer

Deer woke up on a bright summer morning. She found Bear hunting for honey.

"Would you like to play?" asked Deer.

"I'm sorry," replied Bear, "but I haven't had breakfast yet. Help me get this honey, and then I can play."

"Oh, Bear!" sighed Deer. "The buzzing bees scare me."

"Well, then you'd better watch out," Bear told her. "There's a wolf around!"

Deer set off through the woods. "If only I was as brave as Bear," she thought, "I'd have someone to play with."

Suddenly Deer heard a cry. "Help! Help!" called a frightened voice. Deer started to rush toward it.

"Someone's in trouble!" she called, as she passed Bear.

"Sorry," said Bear. "It might be that wolf. I'm scared of wolves."

In a clearing was Rabbit, shivering as the wolf snarled at him.

Deer didn't stop to think. She leaped between the wolf and Rabbit. As she did so, her hoofs hit a hollow log. Boom! The sound echoed through the wood and the wolf fled.

"Oh, thank you, Deer!" smiled Rabbit. "You were so brave. I don't know anyone else who would have done what you did."

"Thank you," said Deer shyly. "I don't suppose you have any time to play, do you?"

"Of course!" said Rabbit.

Kind Little Bear

Little Bear, Squirrel, and Bunny were going out to play.
"Don't go into the river," said Bunny's mom.

"And don't get dirty," said Squirrel's mom.
Bear and his friends played all
morning. At last, Squirrel and Bunny
flopped down in the long grass near the
river. But Bear wasn't tired at all!

"I'm so thirsty!" gasped Bunny.

"I'll get you a drink," smiled Bear. He
splashed into the river and scooped up water in
his big paws.

"I'm so hungry," groaned Squirrel.

"I'll fetch you some nuts," smiled Bear. He scrambled up a
nearby tree, getting twigs and leaves stuck in his wet fur.

"Goodness," sighed Bunny's mom, when they got home.
"You're soaking wet, you bad bear. You've been in the river!"

"Just look at your dirty fur, you naughty bear!" said
Squirrel's mom.

"I was thirsty, so Bear went into the river to get
me a drink," said Bunny.

"Bear got dirty getting me some nuts," added
Squirrel.

Bunny's mom and Squirrel's mom smiled.
"You're not a bad bear at all," they said. "You're
a kind little bear!"

I Love You, Grandma

Little Bear and Grandma were eating breakfast.

"Grandma," asked Little Bear suddenly, "why do I have such sharp claws?"

"To help you find food," came the reply.

"But you told me I have my nose for that," said Little Bear, surprised. "You told me to sniff the air."

"Ah!" said Grandma. "Sometimes your nose leads you to food, but you still have to work to get it."

She took Little Bear to the woods. "Sniff the air!" she reminded him.

Little Bear started to follow his nose. He stopped at a fallen tree.

"I can smell food," Little Bear said. "I can't see it, but I know it's here."

"You'll need to use your claws," Grandma told him. Little Bear dug his sharp claws into the bark. He broke off a small piece.

"Ants!" he laughed. "Delicious!"

"Lunch," smiled Grandma. "Good work, Little Bear!"

"Grandma," asked Little Bear suddenly, "why do I have such a long tongue?"

"To help you find food," Grandma said at once.

"But you told me that I have my nose and claws to do that,"

said Little Bear, surprised.

"Sometimes the best food is hard to reach," Grandma said. She took Little Bear to a clearing. "Smell the air," she said. Little Bear sniffed hard. He lifted his nose.

"Food!" he told Grandma. A huge bees' nest hung from a branch above him.

"I know what to do," laughed Little Bear. He hooked the nest with his sharp claws, lifted it down, and opened it up.

"Honey!" he smiled. "Mmmmm!"

"Supper," said Grandma. But Little Bear's big claws couldn't reach the food.

"So what are you going to do now?" asked Grandma.

"Use my long tongue," laughed Little Bear. And he did!

"How do you know so many things, Grandma?" asked Little Bear suddenly.

"That's easy," Grandma smiled. "When I was small, I was curious... just like you," she said. "You ask so many questions, you'll soon know a lot of things, too." And she hugged Little Bear tight.

"Do you know I love you, Grandma?" asked Little Bear.

"I do!" answered Grandma. She stroked Little Bear's sticky head. "And you know I love you, too," she said.

My Little Kitten

Ella went to visit her grandma every weekend.

Grandma's house was very pretty, with roses growing around the front door and a big yard at the back.

It was also full of cats. A lot of cats.

There was Lady Jane, a white-and-brown cat with very fluffy fur. There was Duchess, a bluish-gray cat with large pointed ears and tiny oval paws. And there was Ella's favorite, Princess Mae, a creamy-colored tabby cat with short, soft fur.

Ella loved to help Grandma look after the cats.

First, her grandma would give the cats their food. Each cat had its own special bowl. Then Ella helped Grandma to groom them. Lady Jane and Duchess needed their long hair brushed at least once every day.

Princess Mae could lick her own fur clean, because it was much shorter. But she still loved to sit on Ella's knee, purring softly, while Ella combed her creamy coat.

Sometimes, Grandma entered her cats in special cat competitions.

They had won a lot of prizes. Ella loved to look at all the photographs and trophies on Grandma's shelf. Her favorite was a large gold cup.

One weekend, Grandma had some exciting news. Princess Mae was going to have kittens!

"Would you like to choose one of Princess Mae's kittens for your very own?" asked Grandma.

"Oh, yes, please," gasped Ella, with shining eyes.

"You'll have to be patient." said Grandma. "The kittens won't be here for another month or so, and then they'll have to stay with their mom until they are around ten weeks old."

Ella's face fell. "Do I really have to wait that long?" she asked.

"I know that seems like a long time, but it will fly by," said Grandma. Ella nodded glumly.

One day, Ella went around to help her grandma prepare for the new arrivals. They had bought a basket and covered it with an old blanket.

"Princess
Mae can have
her kittens in
here," explained
Grandma. "It's
warm and dry, and
she'll feel safe."

Princess Mae
seemed to know
at once that the
basket was for her.

The next time
Ella went to visit, Grandma was waiting at the door.

"I've got something to show you," she said, smiling. "Princess
Mae's kittens have arrived!"

Ella and Grandma crept quietly into the kitchen. There,
curled up beside Princess Mae, were five tiny, furry kittens.

"They were born last night," whispered Grandma.

"They're beautiful!" said Ella softly. "When can I pick
one?"

"Whenever you like," replied Grandma, "but it's best to
wait until they are older, then you'll know for sure which one
you want."

At first, the kittens spent most of their time curled up next
to Princess Mae, drinking her milk or sleeping.

Then, after a week or so, they began to crawl. One stripy
little kitten crawled right across the floor to sniff Ella's hand.

After two weeks, the kittens began
to explore.

Ella was at her grandma's
baking some cakes when the
same stripy little kitten came
over and tried to join in.

When they were four weeks
old, the kittens began to grow teeth.
The stripy little kitten especially loved playing with the red
chewing toy that Ella had bought.

By the time the kittens were six weeks old, they were racing
around and playing with each other. "I think you've chosen
your favorite," smiled Grandma one day as she watched Ella
playing with the stripy kitten.

"I think she's chosen me," laughed Ella. "I'm going to call
her Tiger Mae—after Princess Mae and because she's stripy!
And Grandma, do you think I could enter Tiger Mae in cat
competitions when she's older?"

"Yes," replied Grandma, smiling. "You've learned a lot
about looking after cats. I think that would be a very
good idea!"

"Do you hear that, Tiger Mae?" whispered
Ella. "When you grow up, maybe one
day we'll win a big gold cup, just like
Grandma."

And a little while
later…they did!

Lucky Little Duck

Duck was waddling through the meadow when she met Bunny.

"Hello, Bunny," said Duck.

Just at that moment, something sparkly darted past Duck's head.

"Wow!" said Duck. "Did you see that? It was beautiful! What was it?"

"I'm going to find out," laughed Bunny, hopping off toward the pond.

"Lucky Bunny," sighed Duck sadly, as she waddled after him. "Look at his strong legs. I could never move that fast."

They could soon see the mysterious creature darting around and around above the pond. Then it settled on a tall reed. Duck slipped into the water and paddled quietly toward it.

"Lucky little Duck," sighed Bunny. "I can't swim at all."

"Wow!" whispered Duck, as she reached the reeds. Perched on the tallest reed was the most beautiful creature she had ever seen. Its wings sparkled in the sun. Its body shimmered blue and green.

"Hi," said Duck. "I'm Duck."

"I'm Dragonfly," replied the creature.

"Come and meet my friend Bunny," said Duck. She swam back to the bank.

"We're both lucky—because we have a new friend!" she said to Bunny.

Shy Little Bunny

Bunny's whiskers twitched excitedly as he poked his nose out of his family's new burrow.

"Why don't you see if you can meet some new friends, Bunny?" said his mom.

Bunny scampered off to explore. Soon he heard some voices nearby. He peered through the bushes to see a mouse, a duck, and a squirrel building a den.

"Help me push in this stem, Mouse," said a young duck.

"I am pushing, Duck!" said the mouse.

"I'll help, too," said a young squirrel.

Duck, Mouse, and Squirrel stood back to look at their work.

"It's a good den," said Squirrel, "but it would be better if it had a burrow in it."

Bunny hopped out from behind the bushes. "I'm good at burrowing," he said shyly.

"Really?" said Duck. "Could you help us?"

So Bunny dug a hole inside the den. Then he scooped out a tunnel. Finally, he made a snug little burrow inside.

"Wow!" cried Squirrel.

"The fox will never get in there!" said Mouse.

And Bunny played happily with his new friends outside their new den all day long.

Pussycat, Pussycat

Pussycat, pussycat, where have you been?
I've been up to London to visit the Queen.
Pussycat, pussycat, what did you there?
I frightened a little mouse under her chair.

Silly Sally

Silly Sally swiftly shooed seven silly sheep.
The seven silly sheep Silly Sally shooed shilly-shallied south.
These sheep shouldn't sleep in a shack;
Sheep should sleep in a shed.

Rock-a-bye, Baby

Rock-a-bye, baby, thy cradle is green;
Father's a nobleman, Mother's a queen,
And Betty's a lady, and wears a gold ring,
And Johnny's a drummer, and drums for the King.

There Was an Old Woman

There was an old woman, lived under a hill,
And if she's not gone, she lives there still.

Frisky Lamb

A frisky lamb
And a frisky child
Playing their pranks
In a cowslip meadow:
The sky all blue
And the air all mild
And the fields all sun
And the lanes half shadow.

Frog Went a-Courtin'

Mr. Froggie went a-courtin' an' he did ride;
Sword and pistol by his side.
He went to Missus Mousie's hall,
Gave a loud knock and gave a loud call.

"Pray, Missus Mousie, air you within?"
"Yes, kind sir, I set an' spin."
He tuk Miss Mousie on his knee,
An' sez, "Miss Mousie, will ya marry me?"

Little Lamb

"Baa! Baa!" says Lamb to Mommy Sheep,
"Please can we play hide-and-seek?"

"Where's my lamb?" asks Mommy Sheep.
"Baa! Baa!" shouts Lamb, and out she leaps!

"Baa! Baa!" says Lamb. "I'll hide again—
In the piglets' muddy pen!"

But Mommy finds her right away.
"Baa! Baa!" is all that Lamb can say.

"Baa! Baa!" says Lamb. "I'll hide with my friends."
Mommy says, "There you are with the hens!"

"Baa! Baa!" says Lamb, when the day is done,
"Playing hide-and-seek is fun!"

Little Calf

"Moo! Moo!" says Calf, one sunny day.
"The meadow's where I like to play!"

When a butterfly lands on little Calf's nose,
He says, "Moo! Moo!" and away it goes!

Calf follows the butterfly, calling, "Moo! Moo!"
He sees woolly Lamb and says, "You come, too!"

Just then, little pink Piglet appears,
"Moo! Moo!" says Calf. "We're over here!"

As the butterfly flutters off through the air,
Calf says, "Moo! Moo! It's over there!"

Calf snuggles with Mom when his busy day ends.
He says, "Moo! Moo! I've had fun with my friends!"

The Storm

One night, Lili and Zac were woken up by a big storm.
Thunder crashed and lightning flashed. It sounded very scary.

"I can't sleep," said Zac, opening the curtains to look.

"Nor me," said Lili. They both went downstairs. Mom and
Dad were in the kitchen.

"The storm woke us up," said Zac.

"It's a bad one," agreed Mom. Suddenly the lights went out.

"The electricity's gone off!" cried Lili.

Dad went to get some oil lamps. They all sat drinking hot
chocolate by lamplight and listening to the storm. Then Dad's
phone rang. He looked worried as he talked.

"That was the lighthouse keeper," he said. "The lighthouse

has been struck by lightning. Now it doesn't work."

Dad told them that a boat was trying to come into Karlin Island harbor. "It won't be able to see its way without the light from the lighthouse," he said. "We'll all have to take some searchlights and guide it safely in."

They all made their way to the dark harbor. "First we need to find the boat," said Dad. He shone his big searchlight out to sea. "There it is!" he pointed.

"Oh no!" gasped Mom. "It's heading for the rocks!"

They all stood together and shone the searchlights to guide the boat into the harbor. The boat didn't change direction.

"It's still heading for the rocks!" shouted Zac.

They watched the boat in dismay. Would it see their lights in time?

Then slowly, the boat started to turn around.

"It must have seen us!" Lili yelled excitedly.

The boat followed the searchlights safely into the harbor.

When the captain got out, he came straight over to them. "Thank you so much," he said. "I don't know what would have happened if you weren't here."

"No problem!" said Lili proudly.

Black Beauty Finds a Home

After the kindly cab driver Jerry had to sell me because he had fallen ill began the most terrible part of my life.

First I went to a carter, who overloaded me and wore me out. Then he sold me to a dreadful cab driver called Skinner, who worked his horses until they could work no more. Every day, with no day off to rest, I pulled overloaded cabs, and got whipped for not working hard enough when I was doing my

best. At night I was too exhausted to eat, and I felt so utterly wretched I wished my life would end.

Then one day it nearly did. With four people and a mountain of luggage to haul uphill, and me thin and weak from overwork, my feet slipped from under me. I fell heavily to the ground on my side. I thought I was dying.

"He'll never get up again," I heard someone say. But cold water was thrown over me and eventually I staggered to my feet.

Skinner was persuaded to rest me for a few days, then sent me to another sale. Here, I was put with the old, broken-down horses.

A man and a young boy came and
looked at me. "There's a horse,
Willie, that has known better
days," said the man, patting
me on the neck.

"Could you not buy
him, Grandpa, and make
him young again?" asked
the boy.

I trotted out as well as my
poor, stiff legs would allow.
They bought me, took me
home, fed me hay and oats, and gave
me the run of the meadow in the daytime. By the spring, I was
so much better that they could drive me a few miles, and I did
the work with perfect ease.

One day I was groomed with special care and driven to a
pretty house near
the village. Three
ladies, the Misses
Blomefield, were to
take me on trial.

When their
groom was cleaning
me next morning,
he said, "That is
just like the star

Black Beauty had. And here's the knot in his skin where he was bled, and the little patch of white hair on his back! Why, it must be Black Beauty! Don't you know me? It's little Joe Green, who almost killed you when you were a young horse!" But Joe was a grown man now.

I was driven out each day, and I have now lived in this happy place a whole year. The ladies have promised I will never be sold, so I have nothing to fear. Often, in the mornings, before I am quite awake, I fancy I am still in the orchard at Birtwick where I grew up, standing with my old friends under the apple trees.

Bye Baby Bunting

Bye baby bunting,
Father's gone a-hunting,
To fetch a little rabbit skin
To wrap his baby bunting in.

Hush-a-bye, Baby

Hush-a-bye, baby, on the treetop,
When the wind blows the cradle will rock;
When the bough breaks the cradle will fall,
Down will come baby, cradle and all.

A Star

I have a little sister, they call her Peep, Peep;
She wades the waters deep, deep, deep;
She climbs the mountains high, high, high;
Poor little creature she has but one eye.

Nothing-at-all

There was an old woman called Nothing-at-all,
Who rejoiced in a dwelling exceedingly small;
A man stretched his mouth to its utmost extent,
And down at one gulp house and old woman went.

There Was an Old Woman Had Three Sons

There was an old woman had three sons,
Jerry, and James, and John:
Jerry was hung, James was drowned,
John was lost and never was found,
And there was an end of the three sons,
Jerry, and James, and John!

Old Mother Goose

Old Mother Goose,
When she wanted to wander,
Would ride through the air
On a very fine gander.

I Love You, Mommy

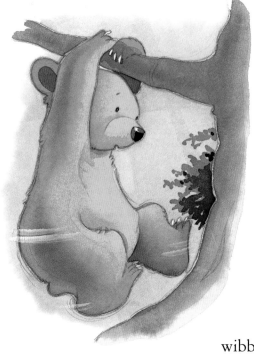

"Look at me, Mommy," called Little Bear. "I'm going to pick that fruit."

"Just a minute," replied Mommy Bear. "There's something you might like to know."

But Little Bear was already climbing the tree.

Mommy Bear saw Little Bear run along a branch.

She saw Little Bear reach out his paw to pick a juicy fruit.

Then Little Bear began to wibble and wobble... *Crash!*

"This doesn't feel like fun!" thought Little Bear.

"Not bad!" said Mommy Bear. "But you look at me now, Little Bear. I'll show you how to climb properly before you go fruit picking again."

Little Bear watched how Mommy balanced as she climbed.

"Your turn now, Little Bear," she said. Little Bear did what Mommy Bear had done.

"This tastes good!" thought Little Bear. "I love Mommy."

"Look, Mommy," smiled Little Bear. "All the other cubs are playing. I'm going to play, too."

"Wait a minute, please," said Mommy Bear. "There's something you might like to know."

Little Bear stopped and turned. "Tell me," he said.

"Be gentle when you play," said Mommy Bear. "Like this." Mommy Bear reached out her paws. She wrapped her arms round Little Bear and rolled him over and over on the ground.

"I love Mommy," thought Little Bear. Then he ran off to play. He did just what Mommy Bear had done. And it felt like fun.

Little Bear was very tired when he got home, but there was something he wanted to say.

"I wanted to tell you," said Little Bear.

"What?" asked Mommy Bear.

"I love you, M…"

But Little Bear didn't finish.

Mommy Bear kissed Little Bear's sleepy head.

"I love you, too," she said.

Lost at Sea

"I'm off to take some photos of basking sharks," said Mom one morning. "Do you two want to come with me?"

"Yes, please!" said Lili and Zac together. They grinned at each other.

Mom got her camera, and then they all got into the boat and set off.

Zac was first to see the basking sharks. "There they are!" he pointed.

"Look at that one. It's leaping!" gasped Lili.

Zac and Lili loved watching the sharks.

Mom took a lot of photos. "I can't wait to go home and print them out," she said happily.

But Mom had been so busy following the sharks, she'd gone too far out to sea. "Never mind, I'll soon find the way home," she told Lili and Zac.

Then it started to get foggy. The fog came down so thick it was hard to see in front of them.

"Oh dear, I think we're lost," said Mom.

Some whistles and squeaks sounded out nearby. Dark shapes bobbed about in the water, at the side of the boat, whistling loudly.

"Dolphins," said Mom.

The dolphins swam around the boat, whistling and leaping out of the water.

"What are they doing?" asked Zac.

"I think they want to show us the way home," said Mom. "I've heard stories of dolphins helping people lost at sea."

Then they heard a familiar clicking sound.

"Whistler!" shouted Lili. Whistler was their favorite dolphin.

Whistler kept very close to the boat. Mom followed him and the other dolphins through the fog until at last Karlin Island nature reserve jetty came into view.

"I think Whistler and his friends guided us home to say thank you for helping him before," Lili said, as they climbed out of the boat.

"I think you're right," agreed Mom.

"You're great, Whistler!" called Zac.

Index

All the Bells Were
  Ringing 103
Amber and the Flowers . . 108
Angel of My Own, An . . . 180
Anna Maria 85
Ant and the Grasshopper,
  The 106
Apple Tree, The 156
Ariel's Song 36
As I Was Going to
  St. Ives. 298
Baa, Baa, Black Sheep . . . 354
Baby Bear's Friend 43
Baby in the Cradle, The . . 336
Bat, Bat 247
Beach Rescue 332
Bed in Summer 167
Bedtime 196
Bella Bunny's Bonnet 28
Bertha Saves the Day 17
Billy and Me 53
Birds of a Feather 187
Birthday Sleepover 170
Black Beauty Finds a
  Home 372
Black Beauty Grows Up . 302
Black Beauty's New
  Owners 338
Bob Robin 174
Bobby Shaftoe 337
Bow, Wow, Wow 246
Brave Billy Bunny 29
Brave Little Deer 356
Broom Song, The 96
Buff 104
Build a House with
  Five Bricks 67
Bunny Helps Mummy . . . 148
Butterfly 127
Butterfly's Ball, The 153
Bye Baby Bunting 376
Can I See Another's

Woe? 174
Candle, A 36
Case of the Carnival
  Crasher, The 300
Case of the Crop Circles,
  The 280
Case of the Disappearing
  Books, The 198
Case of the Disgusting
  Doughnuts, The 218
Case of the Ghost in
  the Attic, The 230
Case of the Stolen
  Necklace, The 254
Cat Came Fiddling, A . . . 336
Cats and Dogs 294
Chairs to Mend 97
Charley Barley 186
Cherry Tree, The 156
Christmas Eve 307
Christmas Tree Fairy 269
Cinderella 144
City Child 117
Clap Hands 285
Clara Cow's Cold 155
Clumsy Fairy 48
Coachman, The 217
Cock Crow 96
Cock Robin's Courtship . . 114
Cold Old House, The 246
Copycat Max 118
Creatures 282
Cross Patch 354
Cuddly Kittens 317
Cut Thistles 194
Dame of Dundee, The . . . 307
Dance to Your Daddy . . . 337
Dibbity, Dibbity, Dibbity,
  Doe 265
Dickery, Dickery, Dare . . 285
Ding, Dong, Bell 216
Dizzy Ballerina Izzy 292

Dolphin Finds a Star 328
Don't Be Shy, Suzy 44
Dove Says, The 175
Dragon Who Was Scared
  of Flying, The 112
Dreams 176
Easter Bunny, The 16
Egg, An 127
Egg Raiders 308
Elsie Elephant's Jungle
  Shower 13
Elsie Marley 115
Elves and the Shoemaker,
  The 56
Emperor's New Clothes,
  The 80
Enchanted Garden, The . . 172
Engine, Engine 104
Fairer Princess Sarah 226
Fairies, The 152
Fairy Seasons 258
Farthing, A 126
Feathers 194
Fidget 175
First 322
Fishes Swim 194
Five Little Ducks 186
Flyaway Fairy, The 347
For Every Evil Under
  the Sun 205
Forever Friends 119
Frère Jacques 216
Friend for Barney, A 162
Frisky Lamb 367
Frog He Would a-Wooing
  Go, A 36
Frog Went a-Courtin' 367
Fudge Won't Play 240
Gee Up, Neddy 322
Georgie Porgie 277
Getting Dressed 343
Gingerbread Men 307

Index

Give Me a Hug! 352
Go to Bed Late 355
Goldy and the Jacket 193
Goldy Locks, Goldy
    Locks. 85
Good Girl, Molly 192
Gossips, The. 104
Grandma's Glasses. 67
Great Brown Owl, The. . . . 65
Grig's Pig. 114
Grumpy Fairy. 128
Hamster Sleepover. 94
Happy Princess Haley . . . 262
Hark! Hark! 323
Hat Like That, A 34
Haymaking. 14
Hazel Squirrel 110
Hearts. 294
Helpful Baby Elephant. . . . 60
Here Comes a Widow . . . 126
Here Is the Church 232
Here We Go Round the
    Mulberry Bush 244
Hey, My Kitten 284
Hickory, Dickory, Dock. . 247
Home Sweet Home 31
How Many Miles to
    Babylon? 233
Hurt No Living Thing 64
Hush, Little Baby. 197
Hush-a-bye, Baby 376
I Bought an Old Man 294
I Eat My Peas with Honey . 14
I Had a Little Hen 37
I Had a Little Horse 24
I Had a Little Nut Tree. . . 157
I Hear Thunder. 342
I Love My Bunny. 89
I Love My Kitten 87
I Love My Pony 88
I Love My Puppy 86
I Love You, Grandma . . . 358
I Love You, Mommy 378
I Saw a Ship 225
I Saw Three Ships 299
I Scream 264

I See the Moon. 205
Ice Cream. 142
Ickle Ockle. 157
If Pigs Could Fly 142
I'm a Big Sister!. 158
In Lincoln Lane 186
In the Treetop. 312
Itsy Bitsy Spider. 246
Jack Sprat's Cat 127
Jacob, the Shyest Rabbit . . 76
Jalissa and the Jewels. . . . 26
Jemmy Dawson 205
Juanita's Big Chance 206
Just as Well, Really! 154
Key of the Kingdom,
    The 296
Kiana and the Butterfly . . . 30
Kind Little Bear 357
Kindness. 143
Kiss It Better 58
Kylee in the Spotlight . . . 234
Lady Moon. 279
Laundry Day 105
Lavender's Blue. 245
Legacy, The 25
Let's Play! 208
Like a Duck to Water. . . . 266
Lion's Birthday 132
Little Betty Blue. 115
Little Bird, The. 323
Little Boy Blue. 53
Little Calf. 369
Little Cottage 232
Little Doll, The. 130
Little Fishes 157
Little Friend 143
Little Husband 306
Little Jack Horner 247
Little Jumping Joan 84
Little Kitten 316
Little Lamb. 368
Little Miss Muffet 84
Little Nag 53
Little Poll Parrot. 24
Little Red Riding Hood . . . 68
Little Sally Waters 277

Little Turtle Dove, The . . 284
Littlest Frog, The 42
London Bells 204
Lost at Sea 380
Lost Billy 242
Lost in the Jungle. 335
Lucky Digger. 286
Lucky Little Duck 364
Lucy Locket. 142
Magical Locket, The 270
Magical Shoes 288
Man Overboard!. 320
Maria's Haircut 50
Mary Had a Little Lamb . 310
Mary, Mary, Quite
    Contrary 126
Maud and the Monster . . . 267
Maxine to the Rescue. . . . 62
Meg Merrilees 137
Merchants of London,
    The 306
Mia's Star Surprise 220
Midnight Fairies, The. . . . 236
Miller of Dee, The 217
Mina's Lucky Shoes 190
Minnie and Mattie 136
Minnie and Winnie 278
Mischievous Mermaids, The 38
Miss Mary Mack 276
Molly Mouse 222
Monday's Child 229
Moon, The 185
Mother Hubbard. 313
Mother Shuttle 295
Mousie 66
Mr Nobody. 277
Mrs Hen 52
Mrs Mason's Basin 66
Mrs White 285
Muffin Man 217
My Best Friend 212
My Black Hen 37
My Dad Is Great. 178
My Grandpa Is Great 120
My Grandma Is Great . . . 140
My Little Cow 205

My Little Kitten 360
My Little Puppy 324
My Maid Mary 97
My Mom Is Great. 260
My Mother Said 166
New Hay 295
Nibbling Neighbors 164
Nickel, A 126
Nothing-at-all 377
Now the Day Is Over 224
O Lady Moon 216
Oh, Bear! 46
Old Farmer Giles 174
Old Mother Goose 377
Old Woman's Three
   Cows, The 15
On the Grassy Banks 355
One Snowy Day 12
Oranges and Lemons 204
Our Baby 265
Owl and the Pussycat,
   The 98
Pat-a-cake 265
Peanut, A 264
Perfect Pony 200
Polar Bear and the
   Rainbow 350
Polly Put the Kettle On . . 264
Poor Peep 256
Pretty Polly 243
Princess and the Pea, The. . 20
Princess Sleepyhead 73
Puss at the Door 105
Puss in the Pantry 97
Pussycat and Robin 195
Pussycat Ate the
   Dumplings 285
Pussycat Mole 355
Pussycat, Pussycat 366
Pajama Party Disco 150
Queen of the Monsters . . . 283
Rain, Rain, Go Away! . . . 252
Rainy Day, The 100
Red Stockings 175
Ride a Cock Horse 66
Ring-a-Ring o'Roses 276

Robin and Pussycat 195
Robins, The 306
Rock-a-bye, Baby 366
Roses Are Red 24
Round-eared Cap 85
Rufus the Farm Kitten 32
Sad Monkey 133
Sam Duckling Swims. . . . 334
Seasons, The 184
See a Pin and Pick It Up . 276
See-saw, Margery Daw . . 115
Showy Ballerina Zoe 344
Shy Ballerina Di 314
Shy Little Bunny 365
Silly Millie Jarter 96
Silly Pig 331
Silly Sally 366
Sing, Sing 15
Skipping 131
Sleep, Baby, Sleep 211
Sleepover Splash 188
Sleepy Baby Tiger 61
Slow Down, Max 74
Slowly, Slowly 323
Small and Pink 78
Small Is the Wren 25
Smoky the Dragon 318
Snoozy Princess Susie . . . 168
Snow White 122
Soccer Fairy, The 10
Song of the Stars 311
Sophie's Baby 274
Sowing Corn 25
Spring 102
Star, A 376
Star Light, Star Bright . . . 232
Storm, The 370
Stranded 348
Sugarplum and the
   Butterfly 54
Sunshine 52
Surprise Sleepover 134
Suzy Helps Out 45
Swarm of Bees in May, A 233
Swing, The 116
Teeth 337

Ten Green Bottles 297
Ten in the Bed 99
Thank You 114
Thank You, Kitty 18
Thaw 52
There Was a Little Girl . . . 84
There Was an Old Crow . 187
There Was an Old Man from
   Peru 14
There Was an Old Woman 366
There Was an Old Woman
   Had Three Sons 377
There Was an Old Woman
   Tossed Up in a Basket. 139
There Was an Old Woman
   Who Lived in a Shoe. . 138
This Is Fun! 209
Thorn, A 354
Three Blind Mice 195
Three Ghostesses 105
Three Little Kittens 177
Tickly, Tickly 67
Tidal Pool Friends 346
Tiger 223
Tiger for Tara, A 319
Tinker, Tailor 233
Tisket, a Tasket, A 37
To the Snail 15
Too Much Sun 253
Twinkle the Tooth Fairy . 248
Twinkle, Twinkle 210
Two Little Dogs 295
Two Little Kittens 72
Two Princesses 40
Ugly Duckling, The 90
Utterly Crazy 156
Wedding, The 322
What a Bad Goat! 330
What Do You Think? 336
Where Are You Going
   To, My Pretty Maid?. . 228
Wind, The 143
Windy's Blowy Day 268
Wise Old Owl, The 187
Yellow Harebells, The 49
You Can Do It, Kitty 19